SEASON'S Blessings FOR YOU

Grace K. Chik

SEASON'S BLESSINGS FOR YOU: A Collection of Christmas Stories

Author photo taken by Dr. Tricia K. W. Woo

ISBN-13: 978-1-77069-082-0

Printed in Canada.

Word Alive Press
131 Cordite Road, Winnipeg, Manitoba, R3W 1S1
www.wordalivepress.ca

Mixed Sources
Cert no. SW-COC-001271
© 1996 FSC
FSC

This book is dedicated in loving memory of
Ferne Isabel Blair
November 1920 - April 2010
A blessed encourager to my creative talents.

Library and Archives Canada Cataloguing in Publication

Chik, Grace K., 1968-
    Seasons blessings for you : a collection of Christmas
stories / Grace K. Chik.

Short stories.
ISBN 978-1-77069-082-0

    1. Christmas stories, Canadian (English). I. Title.

PS8605.H55S43 2010   C813'.6   C2010-905227-7

Table of Contents

Introduction

I STARTED MAKING greeting cards as a hobby in the summer of 1994. At the yearly Canadian National Exhibition in Toronto, a vendor showed two different sets of markers: one changed colours and the other vanished, each when a clear marker overwrote it. This person showed how beautiful cards could be created with these markers. I bought a set each. When I came home, the first thing I did was create a card to congratulate a friend on the arrival of her first baby.

Things started to roll after that. I added stickers, pencil crayons, stencils, embossing tools, colourful stamps, CorelDraw, Microsoft Publisher (and other clipart software), hole punches with different shapes, and many other craft items. I created cards for different occasions and almost all special days. I made them to give to my family, friends, and coworkers. I also made them (and some other paper crafts) by request.

It had gotten to the point where, even though I still could do cards for birthdays, invitations, sympathies, weddings, farewells, and get-wells, I didn't have the time to do all the special days. Thus, I chose to focus on Christmas, because overall it is the time of the year when people are to bless one another.

In the fall of 2002, I was trying to figure out a design for my Christmas cards. I was quietly racking my brain for something unique. Then a thought came into my mind: why not combine two of my favourite hobbies, card designing and story writing? Since then, it has become my format for Christmas cards. I would write a short story and design a cover for it.

The timing of starting a story varied from year to year. One or two started after I completed the production of the current year's card, some might begin anywhere between late winter and early summer, while others commenced only one or two months before the Christmas mailing rush began. It all depended on what ideas the Lord would inspire me to write about.

When the draft was done, I would have it proofread by a friend (for the first few stories) and later by Re-Vision, a critique group within the Word Guild, an organization that connects Canadian Christian writers, publishers, and agents which I am a member of. Then, after the card was in its final format, it would be mass-production time, including stapling the books in the centre and folding them into booklets. For the first few years, it would be done by an office/stationary supply story. Eventually, I did everything myself.

The reaction was phenomenal. Not only were people impressed of my combined talents, many of the recipients were touched by the underlying message of the stories. I heard some shared their cards with their families, friends, coworkers, music students, and even those in need of encouragement. Moreover, a lot of my friends and family members look forward for my card each year.

These are the stories which I have shared with my loved ones. I hope you will be uplifted and blessed, so that you can be a blessing to those who need to be blessed.

Please note: Due to copyright concerns regarding clip-arts, pictures originally used on the covers of my cards are not included in this publication.

2002

MY FIRST STORY was inspired by news stories about people decorating their houses and front lawns in elaborative ways, and especially Christmas comedy films about families declaring war on their neighbours to see who could create the most impressive outdoor home display on the block.

The characters of this story needed to discover that Christmas is a time of sharing, not showing off. Why are we wishing each other "peace on earth" and at the same time trying to outdo one another to be the best?

In 2004, I entered this story to a Christian online Christmas story contest. It came in number ten of the Top Ten winners!

What Would it Take to Have the Best Decorated House?

FOUR MONTHS before Christmas, the people of the little town of Naton were already in a frenzy. Every year, the residents competed for the best-decorated house. They all put their free time into making their rooftops and front lawns into fantastic Christmas exhibits. The judging night was always Christmas Eve. The judge was usually the mayor or a prominent citizen, but this year the identity was kept secret. The winning house would be tax-exempt and receive free government services, such as electricity, for a whole year.

There was an endless clamour of sounds everywhere, from the stores to all the neighbourhoods.

"All right! Who broke a leg off each reindeer?!"

"Why didn't anyone tell me these Christmas lights are no good?!"

"What do you mean you're out of those nutcracker soldiers?! You're supposed to keep track of your entire inventory at this time of year!"

One day, a new family settled in Naton in the midst of the traditional Christmas competition. The Kohowks did their best to live in spite of the ongoing racket. In fact, everybody was so focussed with dressing up their rooftops and front lawns that hardly anyone bothered to welcome them.

ONE MORNING, Mrs. Kohowk went out for a walk. The birds' singing was muffled by the constant bickering and accusations flying around the neighbourhood.

"You stole my idea!"

"Did not! You're just jealous!"

"Turn down that music!"

"Keep your kids and dogs away from my lawn!"

She happened to see a woman dressing a frozen snow-woman in a maid's costume. Her display appeared to be a Christmas dinner party. All the trees and bushes were decked with lights and ornaments. A ping-pong table and chairs were covered thinly with snow. Ice sculptures were shaped and coloured to resemble food, plates, and utensils; only the wine glasses were real. Mannequins in elegant clothes and jewellery sat around the table. Everywhere else, frozen snow-people stood in servants clothes.

Mrs. Kohowk greeted, "Good morning."

The woman turned and studied her. "I've never seen you before."

"My husband, my kids, and I came to live here recently. My name is Marilyn Kohowk."

"Well, nice to meet you. I'm Betty Jones."

Marilyn was impressed of Betty's artistic effort. "Well, you are doing a good job. Did your family help you as well?"

Betty sighed bitterly. "Not as much as I wanted. They're supposed to help me right now but my kids are down with a flu. So my husband drove them to my parents' place out of town and now he still hasn't returned. They always leave things for me to do." Betty glared at Marilyn. "What are you doing here now? If you're thinking of stealing my ideal—"

"Oh, no. My family doesn't have much to decorate our new home; whatever we have is already sufficient."

Betty seemed to accept Marilyn's response. "Okay, I can live with that. Now, if you will excuse me, I can finish this best without any more disturbances."

Marilyn remained friendly. "Certainly. Have a good day."

DURING A LIGHT BLIZZARD on the night of Christmas Eve, Betty was resting in her living room when she heard her next door neighbour shouting outside.

"OUT! GET OUT! YOU'LL RUIN MY CHANCE OF WINNING THE COMPETITION!"

Betty peaked through the small window of her front door. Scampering across Betty's front lawn was a small child in a very warm coat, boots, hat, and mitts.

As the little girl stared in awe at the dinner scenery, Betty was steaming in fury. From her coat closet, she seized a broom. Rushing out the door, she swung her broom at the wandering kid.

"SHOO! GO HOME! YOU'RE TRACKING FOOT-PRINTS AND THE JUDGE WILL BE HERE SOON! GO HOME! NOW!"

As the frightened child hurried towards the next house, Betty's husband rushed out. He took the broom away from his wife.

"Bets, calm down. That was only a little girl. You should have helped her. She might be lost."

"What? And ruin my chance of being congratulated by whoever the judge is? That kid is becoming a menace to the neighbourhood. You're some help, Roger."

MIDNIGHT CAME AND WENT as the blizzard disappeared. Betty was pacing around her living room. Unexpectedly, a sight caught her off-guard. Walking up the road in front of her house was the mayor and the police chief. Neither man took a glimpse at her sculpture. Trailing behind the two men were a group of Betty's neighbours; all appeared to be curious. Quickly Betty grabbed her coat and boots and stepped outdoors.

She managed to catch up to the front of the line. "Mayor Servot. Chief Branz."

The two men glanced at her. "Hello, Betty," greeted Servot.

"Merry Christmas, Betty," greeted Branz.

"Where are you going?"

Branz explained, "The winning house has been found and we're on our way to see it."

As the group continued their journey, more neighbours came out with curiosity. They also wondered why their homes hadn't been judged and when the mysterious judge had made his decision.

They came upon a house at the end of the road. It was decorated with absolutely nothing. Behind the curtains of a large window, one could see the silhouette of a tree with very small lights.

A voice at the back demanded, "How could this be the winning house? We worked so hard at ours and this one has nothing!"

As others raised their voices in agreement, the mayor calmly suggested, "Let's go in and hear what the judge has to say about this one."

They approached the front door. The police chief rang the doorbell. There were light footsteps. They heard the lock click. The door was opened, revealing Marilyn's smiling face.

She greeted, "Merry Christmas, everyone."

Betty demanded, "Marilyn, how can your house be the best-decorated place in Naton?"

Marilyn became puzzled. "I don't understand. My family has no intention of entering the contest."

Servot declared, "Perhaps we can come in and clear the whole matter up."

As the guests entered the Kohowks' household, the neighbours gasped in astonishment. Drinking a cup of hot chocolate in the dining room was the little girl.

Marilyn explained, "My husband found her crying on our front lawn. He took her inside here. Right now he is talking to her parents."

The child turned. Horrified, she placed the cup onto the table and jumped off the chair. She rushed to the mayor and grasped his right leg.

"Those people are mean to me, Mr. Mayor."

Servot patted her head. "I'm sure they didn't mean to be that way, Jessica. You did a good job tonight."

A man who had scolded the child before Betty demanded, "What job? We've been waiting for the judge all night and he didn't show up."

Branz pointed out, *"Au contraire*, the judge did show up but you scared her away."

Everyone, including Marilyn, was surprised and gazed at the frightened girl.

Servot explained, "We, the city council, knew that you were expecting the 'mysterious judge' to be someone with high prestige and popularity. So we decided to send someone who nobody would expect. Jessica's family won last year's contest. I told Jessica that as soon she found the best-looking house, she was to call me at Chief Branz's office. I must say, this indeed is the best-decorated house in Naton."

Branz pointed out, "For the past few years, just about everyone forgot the nature of the contest. It's supposed to be fun. Look what has happened lately. Every day and night, the police force has to keep the town quiet from noisy bickering. There's nothing wrong with the contest itself; it's your attitude towards it. You've been putting so much priority on it that you've forgotten to look after the needs of others. Even when the contest was over, I've heard of a lot of disagreements and broken friendships. It's one thing to make your houses look good on the outside; if you continue to fight about decorating your homes at work, in stores or anywhere, or even within your own families, not only you will make your place a disaster, but also the whole town of Naton. Our town has become a war zone area and there hasn't been much peace around here."

Instantly the crowd's scepticism melted. The once bitter neighbours became saddened by guilt. However, when they gazed at Marilyn's smile they felt a bit of tenderness in themselves.

Servot nodded. "Now look at this house. In fact, can you feel the warmth of this house? There's love in the air. That's what attracted our little judge to choose this place, and that's one of the key ingredients of making this house beautifully decorated."

IN THE SAME WAY, WE CELEBRATE CHRISTMAS BECAUSE GOD HAS GIVEN US THE BEST CHRISTMAS DECORATION FOR OUR LIVES: THE BIRTH OF HIS SON JESUS. OUR LIVES, NO MATTER HOW WE LIVE, ARE MADE BEAUTIFULLY AS GOD HAS INTENDED US TO BE.

I WISH YOU ALL A VERY BLESSED CHRISTMAS AND THE NEW YEAR AHEAD.

2003

I REMEMBER, during my elementary school years, everyone gathered in the gym to sing Christmas carols during the last week of classes before the holidays. On the last day, there would be plays performed by each class. In the afternoon, each class would have a small party and card exchange, as well as present gifts for the teacher. When I was in Grade 6, I became the first person to accompany everyone on the piano with "Twelve Days of Christmas," the only song which the principal didn't know how to play.

There is nothing wrong with getting gifts, but everyone—adult and child—must remember that the only thing more important than possession is life itself.

What Would be Your Christmas Wish?

EXCITEMENT was sensed in a second grade class' party. It was the last day of school before the Christmas holidays.

All the cake, juice, and chips had been eaten. All the favourite carols had been sung. Even the principal, in his traditional Santa Claus role, stopped by to give each child a delightful present.

Ms. Abby had her class sit in a circle on the floor. "Before I wish you off to enjoy the holidays with your families, I would like you to tell me your Christmas wish. I will start as an example. My Christmas wish is someday see all my relatives who live all

over the world. Now, Belinda will continue."

Belinda stood up proudly. "My Christmas wish is to have the prettiest clothes to wear."

Charles stood up. "My Christmas wish is to have the latest Astro-Fighter video game."

Diane got up to her feet. "My Christmas wish is to have a stable of horses."

The game continued. Some wishes were for the ultimate Christmas gifts. Others were rather funny, such as Ivan's wish to be a multi-multi-multi-multi-multi-multi-multi-multi-multi-zillionaire.

There was, at one point, a brief protest when it came to Naomi's turn. "My Christmas wish is to have lots and lots of new clothes."

Belinda angrily stood up. "Hey, you copied my wish!"

"Did not! You said 'the prettiest clothes'!"

"So? That's the same thing!"

Ms. Abby spoke up, "There's nothing wrong with two or more people having similar wishes. Now, let's go on with Oscar's Christmas wish."

Oscar got up to his feet. "My Christmas wish is that my family wins the biggest lottery."

Ivan tried not to protest.

Finally it came to the last pupil, Zenith, who had joined the class very recently. The quietest in the class, he rarely participated in answering Ms. Abby's questions. Though he made a few friends, he was usually alone during recess.

All eyes glared at Zenith, who became speechless by his shyness. Ms. Abby gently encouraged, "It's okay,

Zenith. Share your Christmas wish with everyone, even if it may sound the same as someone else's."

Looking at his tattered shoes, Belinda guessed, "I'll bet it is a new pair of shoes."

Zenith shook his head.

Gregory guessed, "Or a brand new baseball, bat, mitt, and cap."

Again, Zenith shook his head.

Petulia declared, "I know. A one-year pass to the Maxi Movie Theatre."

Ms. Abby urged, "Let Zenith say his Christmas wish. Don't hurry him."

Zenith started with a bit of a stammer. "Well, my Christmas wish is the same wish I have for every day."

Naomi pointed out, "Then, it's *not* a Christmas wish."

Ms. Abby pointed out, "Even an everyday wish is a Christmas wish. Go on, Zenith."

"Well, my Christmas wish is . . . is . . . is . . ."

Everyone leaned forward in anticipation.

Zenith concluded, "Is to try enjoying my life as best as I can."

All the children looked at each other in puzzlement.

Edgar asked, "That's your wish?"

Martin spoke, "I thought it's going to be something like a drum set or the latest Poogie CD."

Ms. Abby gently ordered, "Hold back your thoughts and let Zenith explain his wish to us."

Zenith began, "I don't know what each day will be like. My dad might work at one place for a few days and then search for another job that also lasts just a few days. My mom has a job, but we only see her on Saturdays because of it. My grandparents who lived near a hospital are caring for my baby sister who needs a kidney. In my neighbourhood, there is always some people getting hurt or killed. Although we barely have enough to eat and wear, my parents and I have learned to be satisfied with what we have. The main thing we learned to be satisfied with is our lives. So, that's my Christmas wish: to enjoy my life as best as I can every day."

There was silence as the other kids glared at Zenith in awe. That made him a bit nervous. He glanced at Ms. Abby, who smiled at him.

Sebastien spoke up, "That was cool."

Jenny added, "I agree."

Wendell raised his artificial arm. "More awesome than getting candy."

Zenith blushed happily.

Ms. Abby nodded. "The greatest Christmas wish is to be thankful for your life, and enjoy it the best you can."

DEFINITELY THE BEST CHRISTMAS WISH IS GOD'S BLESSING UPON YOUR LIFE, AND TO BE THANKFUL, REGARDLESS OF THE CIRCUMSTANCES YOU'RE FACING EACH DAY.

"The Lord gives strength to his people;
the Lord blesses his people with peace."

—Psalms 29:11 (NIV)

2004

AT THIS TIME, I chose to focus my stories on the poor and needy, because I do have the heart for the less fortunate. I do whatever I can to help out, ranging from helping to serve hot meals, buying groceries for a food drive, or sponsoring a couple of children from different countries. Occasionally I'd toss some coins to a beggar.

Besides, whenever you give to someone in need, you never know what kind of blessing you'll receive. It may be tangible or just a warm feeling of knowing that you helped someone else.

The Generous Heart of a Beggar

HE SAT AT his usual place on the doorstep of an abandoned convenient store as the falling snow blanketed his body. In front of him was his upside-down baseball hat. Clothed in an old over-sized hooded coat, rubber boots, and thick gloves, he embraced his knees close to his chest. His dark glasses prevented him from seeing much of the scenery ahead of him.

The overall atmosphere was a hurried Christmas season. Children singing Christmas carols stalked their potential audience in hopes of a monetary contribution. Women dragged their husbands and boyfriends into every shop, except those that sold electronics and sports equipment. Businessmen hurried to any available taxicabs or approaching buses. In the midst

of the townspeople's busyness, the beggar was ignored by virtually everyone.

Although some did notice the beggar, their reactions were mostly not warm at all.

"That's what this town needs: a useless bum expecting sympathy!"

"Sooner or later, there will be tramps all over, making this place impossible to attract out-of-town visitors!"

"Get a job!"

"Get a life!"

"Get out of this town! The sooner the better!"

However, not all receptions were as cold as the wintry days. Among those who chipped in a few dollars into the beggar's hat was Charlie, a young office clerk who did more than contribute a small part of his paycheque. Every morning, Charlie would carry a piping-hot portion of leftover dinner to his needy friend.

"Morning, Ren," greeted Charlie as he handed the boxed meal to the beggar.

"Morning, Charlie. Thank you very much. You've been very good to me."

"You're a friend in need. How can I ignore you like the rest of the world?"

"You'll be well-rewarded someday."

"A cheerful morning talk is enough for me."

Whenever he was on his way back to his workplace during his lunch break, Charlie would get Ren a hot take-out meal.

"Charlie," remarked Ren, "someday I will repay you back for your kindness in a way even you would not believe."

Charlie was concerned, thinking his friend would not be able to afford anything from his humble earnings. "Ren, please, I don't want to trouble you."

"You should never doubt my words."

"It's not just that. All I can say is, whenever I find you at your usual spot, you brighten up my day even before my working hours start."

"Like I have said, you should never doubt my words. I will always treasure our friendship."

The only time Charlie didn't get to see Ren was afterhours. Whenever he left to go home, the doorstep of the former store was empty. Charlie could only speculate that his poor friend went to a shelter to have a warm sleep.

Although he was often encouraged by few of his colleagues, many others scoffed at Charlie's generous heart.

"Why do you spend your time and money on wasteful beings like your beggar friend?"

"People like him don't even know how to appreciate things that you give them."

"Your charity will go to waste and you will be left with nothing—just like them. How are they going to help you?"

Like always, Charlie explained, "I cherish my friendship with Ren. You can't put a dollar amount to it because it's worth more than a nice hot meal. Since the day I met him, I knew he wouldn't take advantage of my kindness, because that's one thing true friends don't do."

A WEEK BEFORE Christmas Day, Charlie made his route with a thermos of soup. As usual, he found Ren at his usual place. Charlie handed the thermos to him.

"Morning, Ren."

Ren opened the thermos and sniffed it. "Morning, Charlie. That's a fine soup your wife has made."

"Ren, I was wondering about something."

"About what?"

"Well, I would like to take you to my place for dinner tonight. My wife would like to meet you. Also, you can stay overnight. Could you wait until my day at the office is over?"

Ren smiled. "Sure, I'd love a complete meal for a change."

"Great. See you at lunchtime."

THE EVENING WAS delightful to Ren. As soon as Charlie brought him to his home, Ren was permitted to use the shower. Charlie also loaned him an extra toothbrush and razor and allowed him to borrow his toothpaste and shaving cream. As well, Charlie's wife Sarah gave him a comb for his dishevelled hair. As soon Ren came out of the bathroom in clothes that had once belonged to Charlie's father, the couple was surprised to discover that he was actually much older than he appeared. Ren's face was full of wrinkles and his hair was a mix of white and grey hair.

Ren chuckled, "I love to astound people with my good looks."

Charlie asked, "How could you stand this cold winter at your age?"

"Perseverance, plus your warm food and good friendship."

They ate the simple dinner heartily but silently. During the meal, Ren could sense that something was disturbing both Charlie and Sarah, because they were eating much slower than he was. Their smiles were their attempt to conceal their despair. There was some small talk, but it wasn't enough to break the silence completely.

Finally, Ren commented, "That was a splendid dinner. I really enjoyed it."

Charlie hesitantly spoke, "Thanks, Ren. We greatly sharing what we have with you."

That didn't sound happy to Ren. "What are you talking about, Charlie? What's wrong?"

Sarah explained, "Yesterday, before he left work, Charlie found out that today was his last day. The company went into bankruptcy. He will receive his severance package in the mail, but that could take months with all the legal problems his company is facing now. We've been hoping that Charlie would get the promotion he's been promised." She touched her stomach. "Now we have to afford whatever we can to make our future child happy. I know we will do our best. We can assure you that."

Ren gently demanded, "Charlie, why didn't you tell me this morning or at lunchtime? You know I'm willing to listen."

Charlie shook his head. "I didn't want to spoil our dinner invitation. Besides, you're a great friend to us. But don't worry. I'll continue my daily ritual of delivering your breakfast and lunch to you. I'm not going to abandon you."

Ren patted Charlie's shoulder. "You're very courteous. However, this will be my last night here."

Charlie and Sarah were shocked. "What?!" exclaimed Sarah.

Her husband asked, "You can't leave here."

Ren assured, "Don't worry. It has nothing to do with your unemployment. Surely I can't refuse the goodness of your hearts. Yet, it's time for me to move on to a different place where everyone accepts me, regardless how dirty or unappealing I am. I will never forget your kindness."

Charlie nodded. "We enjoy our friendship with you. That's the best Christmas gift we have now."

Ren shook his head. "Don't be sure about that. Very soon, I will repay you for your kindness in a way even you would not believe."

Charlie tried to dissuade him. "C'mon, Ren, you know—"

Ren waved his scolding finger. "What did I tell you?"

Rolling his eyes upward, Charlie replied, "That I should never doubt your words."

"I will miss you, Charlie and Sarah. You two have been very good to me."

Sarah asked, "Will we see you again?"

Ren shrugged. "Yes, but most likely it will be many years after the birth of your child. I know your baby will inherit your caring hearts."

TRUE TO REN'S words, the next morning Charlie found the guest room empty. He stared into the empty space, remembering the friendly chats he'd had with him. In his hand was a note which Ren left behind. It read:

> *Thank you for being a kindred spirit. I will repay you for your kindness. I promise.*
> *—Your friend, Ren*

His wife approached him from behind and embraced him. "He seemed to be much closer to you than your former colleagues."

"I'm going to miss him. I hope we will hear from him soon."

ON THE AFTERNOON of Christmas Day, Charlie and Sarah heard their doorbell chime. They hurried and opened their front door. Stepping in was a tall slender man in a long dark coat, a furry hat, leather gloves, and shiny boots. In his hands was a white envelope that appeared to be overstuffed.

The man inquired, "Are you Charlie and Sarah Maxwell?"

Charlie nodded. "Yes, sir. Who are you?"

"Allow me to introduce myself. My name is Mr. Derek Fine, attorney of the late Mr. Torrence Sill."

Sarah declared, "I heard about him. Other than running the most successful toy factory, he establishes charities and shelters for the poor and the homeless."

Mr. Fine smiled. "As you can see, his kind heart is noticeable in both cases."

Charlie asked, "And he's dead?"

"He died two nights ago."

Sarah remarked, "How sad."

Her husband demanded, "Did he have anything to do with us? We never met him."

From his pocket, the lawyer pulled out a photo. "Do you recognize this man?"

The couple gasped at the sight of the portrait of the man with a wrinkly face and white and grey hair. Charlie declared, "That's Ren, the beggar."

Mr. Fine chuckled, "Mr. Sill preferred to be called Ren by his friends, especially the unfortunate. For the past six years, around this time, he's been going to different towns dressed the way you've known him. Unfortunately, he never got to stay in a place for more than three days. He always returned home miles from here, unsuccessful. That is, until this year, his seventh year when you befriended him."

Sarah asked, "Why did he do that, Mr. Fine?"

"He was dying and in need of a replacement. Someone with the same kind of generous spirit he had. Maybe bigger than his. He needed someone who can look at any homeless person beyond his or her helplessness. He finally found you and Sarah."

The attorney handed Charlie the envelope. "In his will, Mr. Sill requested to repay you for your kindness in a way even you would not believe. In these documents, he had declared you Vice-President of his toy factory. He has also bought you a nice house and set up an education fund for your coming child. They're all yours with one stipulation."

Charlie's eyes showed hope. "And that is?"

"In your own ways, you will continue to use your generous heart to uplift the unfortunate."

Charlie glanced at his wife's excited eyes before returning his attention to the lawyer. "Of course, we accept."

Mr. Fine smiled. "I'll leave you two to enjoy your happiness. I will call you next month to arrange an appointment to finalize everything. Merry Christmas, Mr. and Mrs. Maxwell."

Charlie joyfully shook the lawyer's hand. "Merry Christmas, and thank you very much."

Sarah nodded. "Have a joyful season."

Bowing to the couple, Mr. Fine left the house.

Charlie and Sarah embraced each other. She remarked, "Torrence—I mean, Ren—was right. This is the best Christmas gift we've got from him."

With tears of happiness, Charlie said, "Thanks, Ren, for your generous heart. We'll never forget you. You will always be a part of our lives."

A LONG TIME AGO, JESUS LEFT THE HEAVEN OF GLORY AND SPLENDOUR TO BE BORN AS A HUMBLE BABY. DURING HIS LIFE ON EARTH, HE REACHED OUT TO THOSE WHOSE NEEDS WEREN'T MET BY

SOCIETY. HIS LOVE ACCEPTS EVERYONE, REGARDLESS OF SOCIAL STATUS.

"Real religion, the kind that passes muster before God the Father, is this: Reach out to the homeless and loveless in their plight, and guard against corruption from the godless world."

—James 1:27 (The Message)

2005

I HAD A HARD TIME putting together this story. I knew it had to be based loosely on the story of Jonah. This story probably had the most false starts that only went as far as half a page before I had to start all over again. I came really close of giving up but had no time to think of any alternative. Finally, I put the story together in time to be distributed to my family and friends.

While it is impossible to be inside a whale, especially since this story takes place in a city, it would be close enough for the Jonah-like character to be with a "whale." (The name Orca means "killer whale," although in the story she has no killer instinct!)

The idea behind the story is this: we are to be a blessing to everyone, even at times when we don't understand why.

Do You Have the Heart to Bless Everyone?

WITH EVERY CAREFUL STEP, three teenagers carried boxes from the Barnabas Centre, a white three-storey, building towards the parking lot. They navigated their feet, making sure they were not walking on ice. They paced more confidently as they reached their cars.

"This has got to be the most unworthy act of kindness," grumbled Jo-hanna.

Anna rebuked, "Stop grumbling, Jo-hanna. There is nothing wrong with providing goods to the less fortunate population of this town. That includes the Broadheart suburbs where we're assigned to go."

Jo-hanna said, "Broadheart appears regularly in the news, but it is for all the wrong reasons: violence, gangs, drugs, murder . . . Well, I think City Hall ought to rename that district Hoodsville. Those bums are making us look bad to the rest of the province." Jo-hanna shook her head, brown curls tumbling down into her eyes. She wanted to help out but hadn't expected to be sent out to the most unpopular place in town.

Dennis pointed out, "There are many families who aren't involved with any serious wrongdoing. Their means of survival can be unpredictable. They don't know when they will end up at the wrong place at the wrong time."

Anna handed her friends a small piece of paper. "Don't forget, we're only delivering these donated goods to the distribution centre where *anyone*, whether the person is peace-loving or trouble-making, can come and get what they need and want. Here's the address."

Jo-hanna stuffed her piece into her pocket. "I can't believe you guys. You actually think those thugs deserve these gifts? They don't know how to be grateful."

"It doesn't matter how they respond," Dennis said. "Everyone deserves to be blessed at Christmas. That's the purpose of the Barnabas Centre, to be a blessing to everyone who doesn't have the necessities to live an abundant life like we do."

After she slammed her car trunk shut, Jo-hanna declared, "I don't know about you guys, but I'm going to take these boxes to another section of town where it is safe and the donations are rightfully deserved."

Anna scolded, "Jo-hanna, we're going to stick with Broadheart. We don't want an overstock in one area and a shortage in another. If you're not comfortable with Broadheart, let us take the boxes from you."

Jo-hanna shrugged, then shook her head. "Oh, all right!" she said, begrudging the very words. "I still think I ought to check the other distribution centres to see if they need a few extra donations."

JO-HANNA HAD only driven a short distance away from Bartholew Centre when the wind picked up speed, rapidly sending countless snowflakes in all directions. Her windshield wipers couldn't clear her view. She slowed down, hoping she wouldn't hit any pedestrians. She could barely see the blurry traffic lights.

What's happening? she thought. Why has the weather gotten worse? This wasn't part of today's forecast.

As she carefully turned at a corner, Jo-hanna suddenly noticed a woman cautiously walking along the sidewalk. Her feet slid, but she avoided a fall by stepping off the sidewalk onto a patch of gravel.

Excitedly, Jo-hanna rolled down the passenger's window and honked a few times. "Ms. Orca! Ms. Orca! It's me, Jo-hanna! Wanna lift?"

Ms. Orca squinted for a few moments. Eagerly, she hurried to Jo-hanna's car and got in. "Thanks, dear. I'd rather be in a car than walking outside."

Jo-hanna drove on. "I'm glad to see you. I've not seen you since I graduated from junior high."

Ms. Orca chuckled, "You were my best math student."

"So, where have you been?"

"I've moved to a small apartment not far from here. I'm now teaching at a nearby elementary school."

Jo-hanna shook her head in confusion and ruefully chuckled, "You'll have to help me out. I'm not familiar with the area, and with all this snow, I'm not even sure where I am exactly."

"We're not too far from Broadheart."

Jo-hanna was stunned. "*What?!*"

She parked her car at a roadside and faced her former teacher. "You lived in Broadheart?"

Ms. Orca placed her hand on Jo-hanna's shoulder. "I understand your reaction. It's unfortunate that this once peaceful neighbourhood has picked up some bad habits."

"Why did you move here?"

"Three years ago, my ex-husband gambled away our mortgage money. After my divorce, I had to sell my car. I needed the money for rent."

"Isn't it risky to live here?"

Ms. Orca nodded. "You bet. A few times my son and I came very close of being casualties. I have a few friends who are either recovering from their wounds or didn't survive at all."

"How could you live in this neighbourhood with such a bad reputation?"

"You would have to make the best not only for yourself, but also for your neighbours, including those who are causing trouble. You have to demonstrate to them that you care about them. I don't know how long it's going to take, but someday your acts of kindness and those of others will turn this neighbourhood around for the best."

Ms. Orca looked through the windshield as the wind died down. "Listen, Jo-hanna, do you mind if we stop by at that building over there? I need to pick up a few things."

Although stunned, Jo-hanna started her car. "Yes, sure. What address is that?"

"1463 Redeemed Ave."

From her pocket, Jo-hanna unfolded a small piece of paper. Written in ink was the address "1463 Redeemed Ave."

"The distribution centre," spoke Jo-hanna.

Ms. Orca gave her a quizzical look. "You need some things from here as well?"

Jo-hanna shook her head. "I've got some things I need to unload. How about giving me a hand?"

MAY THIS SEASON BE A BLESSING TO EVERYONE AROUND YOU, INCLUDING THOSE IN NEED.

"I'm telling the solemn truth:
Whenever you did one of these things to
someone overlooked or ignored,
that was me—
you did it for me."

—Matthew 25:40 (The Message)

2006

BEFORE 2006, my stories were almost four pages long (one sheet, folded in half). I took a chance on this particular year to be free and expand the length of my composition as long as I could. It was also my first story to show reflections of a character's past. By far, it turned out to be the longest Christmas story I have written. To my amazement, the feedback I got suggested the recipients enjoyed the story, and some were touched by it.

The story was based on Charles Dickens' *The Christmas Carol.* The main difference was that the Scrooge-like character lost her money to her so-called friends (contrast that to the actual Scrooge's gain of money at others' expense). Also, one character reflected Christmas Past, Christmas Present, and (to some degree) Christmas Yet-To-Come all at once. The focus I wanted to bring out of the story was this: the only way to have real peace and trust is to forgive.

A Carol of Mercy

ALTHOUGH SOMEWHAT QUIETER than the rest of the year, a medical clinic was full of activities on every floor. There were a few small groups of carollers walking quietly in search of lonely patients to listen to some Christmas favourites. Many patients had families and friends visiting to wish them well. Once in awhile, an ambulance or someone from a charity organization brought in a homeless person either for medical attention or to seek temporary shelter from the cold.

It was early afternoon on Christmas Eve when a little girl escorted a coughing woman in baggy clothes into the clinic's reception area. The few nearby doctors and nurses hurried towards them; two of them seized an idle gurney.

One doctor proclaimed, "My goodness, Eugeena. You nearly froze to death!"

Despite her coughs, the woman scolded, "Don't prolong your greetings, Dr. Reeman. I'm sick and cold!"

As two other doctors heaved Eugeena onto the gurney, the little girl asked, "Auntie Eugeena, can you join my mommy, my daddy, and me for Christmas tomorrow? Mommy says that you can stay as long as you like, even after New Year's Day."

Eugeena continued to cough throughout her response. "Lisa, you tell your mommy, 'No, Thanks.' I'm in no condition to celebrate this nonsense."

Dr. Reeman ordered, "Take her to Room 24. It's the only private room available."

As the doctors and two nurses pushed Eugeena into the halls, another nurse grabbed her coat. "I'm walking Lisa home. I know where she lives."

When the reception area regained its quietness, a lone African nurse picked up the phone and dialled. She waited briefly.

"She's here."

"EXCEPT FOR THAT nagging cough, you're fine, Eugeena," declared Reeman to Eugeena, whose hospital robe enhanced her skinniness. "It should go away by tonight."

Coughing a few times, Eugeena remarked, "That's good news?"

Hesitantly, he commented, "You should have accepted your little friend's invitation. You shouldn't be too harsh with your reply. Besides, a longer stay at someone's home guarantees you better hospitality than what we can do for you here."

Eugeena shrugged, "Her mother is my best friend I can trust. The girl is definitely a carbon copy of her generosity. But then, I can't go into anybody's home. It will remind me of everything I have lost. Through trust."

"How did she find you today?"

"Lisa must be born with a tracking system in her brain. School must have let the kids out. She found me hobbling through Demeter Park; it's not even her usual route to her home. I know that because a year ago she gave me her address and phone number. She must have told her mother that she found me, loitering everywhere in this town."

Heading to the door, Reeman said, "I'll leave you alone now. I'm to check in on my other patients. If you need anything, push the reception button near your bed. Feel free to take the donated clothes in our storage room down the hall. Merry Christmas, Eugeena."

As she laid down, Eugeena muttered, "Why should anyone be merry when there is no trust?"

MOMENTS LATER, Eugeena heard a gentle knock on the door and slowly sat up as the African nurse appeared.

"Good evening, Eugeena. I hope I didn't wake you up."

Eugeena gazed warily at her. "To tell you the truth, I can't sleep at all. Who are you?"

The nurse brought a vacant chair closer to Eugeena and sat down in it. "I am Wendy. I was wondering if we could have a talk."

"About what?"

"For starters, I'd like to get to know you more. I was transferred to this clinic a few months ago. I heard from the other nurses about you coming here on Christmas Eve for the past three years."

"Christmas is the most distrusting time of the year. This is the only place I can go without feeling too disturbed about it."

Wendy urged, "Tell me about yourself."

"Where should I begin?"

"Anywhere you wish. I can tell you haven't told a soul about something terrible that happened to you a few years ago."

Eugeena thought for a moment. "I was born to a rich, prominent loving couple. My parents were president and vice-president of the same head office of a bank. The only other person in the household was Fran, our housekeeper; she was hard-working and very caring. We had a lavished lifestyle. You know, we went on trips to Europe, Asia, the Caribbean, and Australia every year, dined in expensive restaurants once a month and wore the latest style of clothes. But what impressed me the most about my parents was the fact that they gave away more money than they spent. They sponsored children in poor countries to get good clothes, education, and medicine. They donated money to homeless shelters and helped anyone in financial need without question.

"My father died when I was five and my mother was immediately promoted to president. Still, the three of us went on happily with our lives. That is, until two years later, the last day of school before the Christmas holidays."

"I have some bad news, child," declared Fran as young Eugeena entered.

Eugeena looked around the hallway. "Where's my mommy?"

"That's where the bad news comes in. Early this morning, the police came into your mommy's office and took her to jail for using the bank's money wrongly."

"What?! Mommy wouldn't do that!"

"I believe that too, child. Right now your mommy has lots of lawyers to find the truth behind this accusation."

"What's going to happen to us?"

"Things have already been arranged. After we spend some time with your mommy in prison on Christmas Day, I have to send you to the Eleos Boarding School for Young Girls. Then I have to attend my sick father who lives not too far from here. I'll keep in touch with you about your mommy."

Eugeena tearfully threw her arms around her. "This is going to be my first lonely Christmas without you and Mommy!"

Fran caressed the girl's back. "There, there, child."

"The boarding school," continued Eugeena, "was a big contrast to what I had heard about those places in general. The overall atmosphere was very bright. The teachers and headmistress were nice. Lots of facilities, including a library, exercise room, indoor swimming pool, cafeteria, snack bar, arcade, and a bookstore."

"And the other girls?" asked Wendy.

Eugeena's smile morphed into a frown. "Almost all the girls avoided me a few days after I arrived. They kinda knew me through rumours as 'the daughter of the latest embezzler.' They sort of ignored me throughout my stay."

"You said *almost* all the girls," reminded Wendy. "Someone must have ignored all the rumours to make friends with you."

Eugeena nodded. "Her name is Joy, my best friend. She later became the mother of Lisa. From the day I met her, she has been the only person, other than Lisa, who has my trust."

"Hi, there," greeted a blond girl at a corner of the snack bar.

Eugeena pouted, still unable to come to full terms with her mother's arrest. "What do you want?"

"Look, Eugeena, it's going to be all right. I just wish the other girls would forget about the rumours and make friends with you. I even tried to talk to them, but no one listened."

"Well, thanks for standing up for me."

"I want to do more than that. I want to be your friend."

Eugeena glared at her. "Oh, really?"

The girl nodded her head. "My name is Joy."

Eugeena smiled for the first time since entering the boarding school. "How do you do, Joy?"

"If it weren't for Joy, I would always be lonely and miserable. She even invited me to her home for long weekends, Christmas holidays, and summer vacation that year."

Wendy asked, "How was your mother's trial?"

"My only source of info came through Fran, whenever she called me. The trial was a closed door type, which meant there was no media allowed. From what I gathered from her, the prosecution was pouring out a lot of evidence about my mother being a criminal. Her lawyers were doing their best to prove them false. It seemed to me that the trial would never end. But that thought died on the last class of the last day of school before summer began."

The classroom door opened slowly. All heads turned as Fran and a well-dressed woman entered. Excitedly, Eugeena hurried towards them.

"Mommy! Fran!" exclaimed as she hugged both of them.

Fran explained, "We bring you good news, child. Your mother has been found innocent of the crime she's been wrongly accused of."

Eugeena asked, "Do they know who did it?"

Her mother answered, "My own assistant, whom I have trusted with all my business affairs, felt snubbed when she didn't get my former position. She figured she could get her revenge by framing me so she could get my current job. Now she has a lot to explain when her time in court comes. We're here to take you home and celebrate."

Eugeena's mother tilted her daughter's head slightly upward until their eyes met. "Honey, be careful when you meet people. Nowadays, it's hard to know who is genuine and will not take advantage of your goodwill. It's unpredictable when someone robs you of your trust."

Happily, Eugeena beckoned Joy to her side. "Mommy, can Joy join our celebration?"

"We'll talk to her mother when she comes and invite her as well. By the things you've been saying to Fran about her, Joy is very worthy of our trust and friendship."

"Yay!" shouted the girls as they hugged each other.

Eugeena chuckled, "My friendship with Joy has practically lasted forever. I went back to my old school but kept in touch with her. We took turns inviting each other for dinner or whatever. She skipped a couple of grades and finished university two years early. I witnessed her saying her wedding vows and I was there a few days after she gave birth to Lisa. We consistently contacted each other. That is, until four years ago."

"What happened at that time?"

"Someone betrayed my trust, which set my life on a downward spiral. It also depleted my joy for all the Christmases from then on."

"How did it start?"

"Four years earlier, at the beginning of my university years, I met a wonderful guy named Quinton. We dated for three years. He brought me into his circle of friends and I joined their activities, like skiing, baseball games, and nightclubbing. Of course, we had many romantic times together. I really loved him and I thought he loved me, too. During our last year of study, he seemed to be preparing us to live together in the near future."

"Seemed?"

"Well, I don't know why at that time, but he really wanted this enormous mansion."

"This is the house, girl," declared Quinton, a tall and slender young black man, as he handed her a real estate printout at a private corner of a coffee shop. The house appeared to occupy the entire block. A high black gate stood in front of the vast lawn.

"Ten bedrooms?" asked Eugeena. "Why would we need ten bedrooms? Besides, I was hoping for a normal house with four or five bedrooms. This is too big for the two of us."

"But it's the best house in town. Look what else it has: a home theatre room, a recreation room, a dance and banquet hall that can hold a hundred people."

"And look at how much it costs: fifteen million dollars! That's almost my entire savings. You expect me to spend my entire fortune on this? Quinton, be reasonable. Think of the property taxes."

"I already talked to the owners. They're willing to bring the cost down to fourteen million five hundred thousand. Besides, I've got everything figured out. You pay half and I'll pay the rest. Of course, I'll be paying so much per month."

"I don't know. I wish you would talk to me first."

"C'mon, it's going to be a great investment for the future."

"A great investment is done through the heart, not through the wallet. Please, Quinton, reconsider this. Please?"

Eugeena shook her head, "This went on for weeks. I kept begging him to find a smaller house and he kept insisting on that mansion. Finally, for whatever reasons, I gave into his pleadings. However, after he paid a few thousand dollars, he asked me to help him. He claimed that his job at a local coffee shop had reduced his salary. After I forked over the money to pay the remainder of the house, we didn't see each other very much."

"Because you were busy with your studies?"

Eugeena shrugged. "That was my initial thought. I e-mailed him a lot and left messages on his answering machine. He called back a few times, but those talks were brief and informal. No romantic stuff. Also, when I went to look for him at the coffee shop, his coworkers told me that he had quit a few days after the house was fully paid for.

"Then, I got an invite for the Christmas Day party at the house which he was renting. His circle of friends was there, plus a woman whom I had never seen before. Two things were unusual about her. One, Quinton was very cozy towards her. Two, she had a peculiar tattoo."

Amidst the chatter and laughter in the living room, Eugeena sat quietly by the burning fireplace. With a small glass of juice in her hand, she gazed suspiciously as Quinton nuzzled his cheek against a brunette woman's back. A tattoo of a large black spider was displayed on the back of her right hand; above the spider were the letters 'LH' and below it was a red teardrop which was half its size. The woman's giggles fuelled Eugeena's curiosity.

Why is Quinton with her instead of me? she pondered.

Finally Quinton stood up and clanged his glass. "Excuse me, everyone. First of all, I want to thank you for coming here for this occasion and to wish you a Merry Christmas. Second thing I want to announce is it's my pleasure to announce my engagement to the love in my life, Kalee!"

As Kalee rose and kissed Quinton, only the horrified Eugeena didn't join in the applause and cheers. Standing up furiously, she splashed her remaining juice onto his face.

"You swindler! Is that why you kept insisting on that house?! What kind of an investment for the future is that?!"

"An investment for our future. That is, Kalee and me. By the way, I managed to bring the cost down to fourteen million flat."

"What did you do with the five hundred-thousand?"

With a British accent, Kalee teased, "Well, you should know how expensive the new furniture and everything else for the house is, plus the stuff we need to get for the wedding."

Quinton snickered, "Besides, we couldn't let that money of yours sit idly in your accounts and do nothing, like the way many rich people would do with their money."

Eugeena demanded, "We? Who do you mean by 'we'?"

Quinton explained, "We call ourselves the Sherwood Forest Gang. I'm like Robin Hood,

Kalee is Maid Marian, and these guys are my Merry Men. To us, you're one of King John's people."

As more laughter filled the room, Eugeena slapped Quinton's cheek. "The real Robin Hood would at least give to the poor, not horde everything for himself and his gang."

Quinton shrugged, nursing his sore cheek. "So what? We don't have to follow the characters to every detail."

Tears streamed down Eugeena's face. "All these times we spent together meant nothing to you. You're no longer the man whom I once enjoyed being with."

Quinton ordered, "Out of here, peasant girl. You don't belong here anyway . . . or anywhere."

As more laughter rang out throughout the house, Eugeena dashed to the front door. She just put on her coat and boots when Kalee, snickering, called, "One more thing, Eugeena."

Although she didn't turn around, Eugeena felt a card being slipped into her coat pocket.

"Here's an invitation to our wedding," explained Kalee. "You should recognize the address; it's the new house which you have 'bought' for us. Oh, if you decide not to show up, don't bother to reply."

Without another word, Eugeena hurried out, slamming the door behind her. She hurried a few blocks away. When she rested at a street corner, she fished out the invitation. On the top right corner were the words "To: Eugeena." Below it was a photo of Quinton and Kalee in their wedding outfits; her tattoo was very visible. In despair, she shoved it back into her pocket.

A tear flowed down Eugeena's cheek. "'You don't belong here anyway . . . or anywhere.' Those words rang in my head ever since. They troubled me everyday; I couldn't even get a good night's sleep. He literally cursed me with those words. Just like my mother, I had been plagued on Christmas."

Wendy remarked, "They're the reason why you couldn't settle down or even go to someone's place for a meal."

Eugeena nodded. "As you can imagine, I went berserk. For the remaining Christmas holidays, I locked myself in my room and did nothing but cried. I wouldn't talk to anyone, not even my roommates, although they did somehow find out what Quinton did. As if I were dying, I sold everything I had, paid all my credit cards and closed all my back accounts. I ate very little each day. I didn't go out anywhere because I was afraid to see Quinton and his so-called 'merry gang.'"

Wendy approached Eugeena and embraced her. Unable to hold back her tears, Eugeena wept soundly.

The nurse assured, "It's okay to let those tears out, Eugeena. Those painful memories need to come out."

"I thought I was careful before I put my trust on Quinton. My mother told me to be very careful about people before confiding in them."

"I'm sure you were. Unfortunately, the saying is true: 'the more you know about someone, the more there is to know about them.' I'm certain you did your best to get to know Quinton."

As soon Wendy released her, Eugeena continued, "In mid-January, I fled the city with nothing but the clothes on my back, one knapsack full of my only belongings, and whatever cash I had emptied from my accounts. For almost eleven months, I drifted from place to place, slept on sidewalks and parks if I was allowed, and received food and shelter from drop-in centres, if I was lucky. I didn't give myself into booze, drugs, and bad relationships. Twice, I came close to becoming a victim of crime but, fuelled by my anger against Quinton, I nearly cracked those hoodlums' jaws, wrists, backs, and ankles.

"When I first heard about this place offering free shelter, I started to come here every Christmas Eve and stay put until one week after New Year's Day. For the rest of the year, I wandered around. I can never settle down to any place I would call home."

"What do you think happened to Quinton since that fateful day?"

Eugeena sneered, "Who cares about that con artist? He and his wife are probably living in the lap of luxury in that house he bought with my money. Their lifestyle is carefree of all money problems . . . and careless for people like me."

Wendy took a deep breath. "Actually, they didn't get married."

"What?"

"There was a wedding, but they didn't end up as husband and wife."

"How did you know? You don't even know Quinton."

"I do know him and I was at his wedding."

"Dearly beloved," began the justice of the peace as he stood in front of Quinton and Kalee and hundreds of guests under an enormous tent in the backyard of the mansion, "we're gathered here to watch these two individuals be joined as husband and wife. If there's anyone amongst us who has reasons for them not to be married, let him speak up or forever hold his peace."

At once a police chief and two of his officers hurried in. "We'll do the honour."

As people gasped in horror, Kalee attempted to flee to the back of the tent. However, more officers from all entrances blocked her. One of them seized her right hand and examined its back.

"Chief Torry, take a look."

The chief glanced at Kalee's hand. "Well, madam, looks like you alone will be spending your honeymoon back in London as soon your extradition goes through. I'm sure you'll be happy to be reunited with your cronies."

Kalee squirmed as officers handcuffed her. *"I didn't think we were known in this country."*

"Apparently, we had no idea about you or your gang," explained Torry. *"That is, until recently."*

Quinton demanded, *"Chief Torry, what's going on with her?"*

"Let me ask you this: what did she tell you about the initials 'LH' on her hand?"

"It's to remember an old boyfriend who loved to collect spiders."

"Oh, really? Well, we checked with the London police and they told us that none of her seven husbands whom she killed for the past ten years had 'LH' as their initials."

Quinton became overwhelmed. *"Seven husbands? Murdered?"*

The chief nodded. *"I'm afraid so, son. 'LH' stands for 'Latradectus Hesperus,' the Latin name for black widow spiders."*

As everyone reacted in horror, Torry continued, *"This*

lady is part of the Black Widow Spiders, a gang of female killers in London. They marry rich fellows and arrange fatal accidents for their unsuspecting husbands during their honeymoons. Your so-called bride is the last one to be caught."

Glancing at Kalee, the chief remarked, *"I kinda don't blame you for falling in love with her. She may appear to be twentysomething, but she's actually forty-eight."*

Kalee screeched, "How dare you, revealing my age in front of all these on-lookers!"

Torry calmly ordered, "Take her away and read her rights."

As the police dragged her away, Kalee screamed, "This place would have been mine! All mine!"

He patted the distraught groom. "I'm sorry for this to happen on your special day. If it's any comfort, you're the only victim of this gang of femme fatales to survive. I do hope you'll recover from this."

Ignoring the guests' murmuring amongst one another, Quinton watched as the police chief left. With all his might, he tried to suppress his tears. He looked upward as if he was looking for a way to repent.

Wendy continued, "It turned out that someone who had met Kalee weeks before the wedding had been a little suspicious about her tattoo and did some research on the Web. Through her findings, she called the police."

The nurse took a deep breath. "Quinton pleaded for everyone to leave him alone. Some of us tried to ask him what was wrong, but he was too distraught over Kalee's deception. On that night, he couldn't enjoy the luxury he had stolen from you. The whole series of events, from the day he started to con you into buying the house, harassed his conscience daily. He remains to this day in remorse. Even those same words, 'You don't belong here anyway, or anywhere' haunt him constantly. A few weeks later, after he sold the house, he came to your former residence to patch things up with you. However, your angry roommates chased him away. In desperation, he came to live with me, confessed what he had done to you, and begged me to help him look for you."

Eugeena became indignant. "Who are you to him? His new wife?"

Wendy shook her head. "I'm his sister."

Eugeena didn't take the revelation too kindly. "Well, is that why you're here with me? And excuse me for speaking unkindly about your selfish sibling."

"I can assure you, Eugeena, I'm not here to take advantage of you the way Quinton did. I don't blame you for harbouring ill thoughts about him."

"So, what is it like to have a con man for a brother?"

"I was shocked, too, for the deception he had gotten himself involved with."

"What do you mean by that?"

"Since we were kids, Quinton had participated with his friends in many harmless pranks on others, mostly girls. Before they entered university, they decided to scam a rich student; so, they chose you and Quinton was to lure you into surrendering most of your money. What his friends didn't anticipate was the fact that Quinton was falling in love with you. If his friends hadn't interfered, Quinton very likely would have married you and lived in a normal house like you hoped for. To remind him of their original plan, they found Kalee, who persuaded them to let her be part of the gang. It was her idea to trick you into buying the house and then marry Quinton herself. That big house was meant for him, Kalee, and his friends to live together in luxury. Those boys had no idea that she was a serial killer; she would probably have killed them all if their wedding had gone on. They, too, have regretted what they did to both you and Quinton."

Eugeena demanded, "Why is he looking for me? To make fun of me for what I look like now?"

"No."

"To use another scheme on me so he could take what I have left?"

"No."

"Well, I'm not going to be his bait in snaring another unsuspecting rich victim."

"You're not going to, because those aren't his reasons for seeing you."

"Well, what are his reasons?"

"One, he wants to apologize for what he did to you. Two, he wants to return to you all your money which he stole. Three, he's dying and it would be meaningful for him to see you again."

Eugeena rolled her eyes upward in disbelief. "Oh, great. He has you conned, too, into thinking he's dying, so he can get your pity to help track me down."

"He began to feel extremely ill and weak two years ago. As a nurse, I arranged to have him tested twice to be sure. He has ALS, also known as Lou Gehrig's disease. We didn't know whether he would still be alive if and when I found you."

"What does he expect me to do when he sees me?"

"He expects nothing from you, but what he wants you to do is forgive him."

"Forgive him? Are you kidding? That scheming brother of yours gave me misery that continues to this day!"

"He did upset you terribly, but you should know that running away won't ease the pain. Not only do you need self-worth and self-esteem back in your life, you also need peace to break out of the ongoing anger, bitterness, hurt, and resentment you harbour against my brother. Not only is it the best medicine, but forgiveness can also help you to restart your life. Besides, would it be better to accept his apology when he is alive than wish you had after he's dead?"

Shortly after, they heard a light knock on the door. Wendy assisted Eugeena off the bed and on the chair.

Eugeena demanded, "What am I doing on this chair?"

"It would be best for you to see Quinton on the same eye-level."

Wendy hurried to the door and opened it. She stepped aside as the young man entered slowly on his motorized wheelchair. He wore a long loose coat over his pyjamas; oversized shoe-like slippers covered his feet. His right fingers barely touched the keypad as he moved closer to the astonished Eugeena. Attached to the back of his wheelchair was a breathing apparatus shaped like a fire-extinguisher. From the machine, the end of a clear plastic tube was fastened to both his nostrils. His left hand clutched a white envelope.

Wendy walked to a corner to watch. Although his speech was slow and slurred, his words were clear.

"Eugeena, it's nice to see you again."

Eugeena softly asked, "Quinton, is that really you?"

He nodded feebly. His shaky right hand reached towards her face. She leaned closer to him. His fingertips gingerly felt the smoothness of her cheeks. His thumb caressed her lips. When he gazed at her eyes, he felt a tear running down his cheek.

"Eugeena, you look as beautiful as the day we first met."

Eugeena, trying to hold back her tears, giggled and blushed.

"Eugeena, I want you to know that I'm truly sorry for ruining your life. I'm not the same man whom you were bitter about for the last few years. Will you please forgive me?"

She wiped her tears. "Of course, Quinton, I forgive you."

Summing up as much strength as possible, he handed her the envelope. "This is your money, plus interest. Take it back and use it to rebuild your life."

She gently clasped her hand around his. "As soon I settle down and find a job, I'll help you to find the best medical facility that specializes in ALS. This is how true wealthy people use their money."

Quinton nodded. "I know that now. Thank you."

He rolled his wheelchair backwards. "Excuse me, but I have an appointment with my specialist at the other side of town. My sister will give you my e-mail address and pager number. I'd like to keep in touch with you."

"I'd like that, too. Merry Christmas." For the first time, Eugeena felt at ease to utter those last two words without a hint of bitterness.

"Merry Christmas," he said.

Smiling, Wendy opened the door to let her brother through. She waved at Eugeena, who waved back.

In haste, Eugeena seized the phone beside her bed. With her fingers fishing into one pocket, she pulled out her small red coin purse. Opening it, she brought out a small scrap of paper. She rapidly dialled the number, then anxiously waited.

"Hello? Is that you, Joy? . . . Yeah, it's me. . . . Yeah, Merry Christmas. . . . Hey, listen. I don't mean to barge in or mess up your plans but, is dinner still on tomorrow?"

"Blessed are the merciful, for they will be shown mercy."

—Matthew 5:7 (NIV)

2007

2007 STRETCHED ME more than ever before. Instead of one, I wrote three stories. It might be hard to know for sure, but it might be interesting to note that those who received my cards might or might not have realized that different people got a different story.

Be Bad No More is the story of the Three Little Pigs, written from a different perspective. In this story, the pigs react differently when the wolf seeks redemption from them. Don't worry, there were no pigs fleeing or being eaten, no houses blown into pieces, and no boiled wolf.

One More is based on the Biblical parable of the Lost Sheep. Only one person cared enough to go out and look for his wayward employee. The "poor and needy" theme isn't just limited to the homeless. Every one of us has even a slight hint of the feeling, whether it's financially, socially, mentally, emotionally, or health-wise.

In *Santa's Deliverance*, a man who dresses up as the jolly man to cheer up children receives an unusual request. Little does he know that the request will bring closure to his lifelong regret.

Be Bad
No More

IN A SMALL TOWN lived the Pig family with three children. Their names were Pearl, Isaac, and Giselle. Throughout their childhood, they were very happy.

But the only aspect that brought misery to the siblings was their classmate Wolfie. Everyday, he would taunt all his classmates without end or mercy. His favourite targets seemed to be the Pig siblings.

He splashed mud at Pearl's dress. "There! That looks much better."

He tied Isaac's tail to a pole at every race and relay. "See ya at the finish line!"

He tripped Giselle's weak leg. "You're always too slow, you lame Pig."

After every torment, he always ended with, "You'll never be as great as I'm going to be! Some day I'm going to be famous and everyone will look up to me!"

Teachers tried everything to discipline Wolfie. They had him return whatever he had stolen or replace whatever he had ruined; however, those things would be either taken away or messed up again. They had him write repetitive sentences, promising not to misbehave again (it turned out he forced his victims to do it for him). They also ordered him to say encouraging words to his classmates; instead, he belittled them.

His parents were not pleased with Wolfie's behaviour, but they did very little to punish him. Whenever the school reported his misdemeanours, his father would give him a long lecture about respecting others while his mother would look on with disdain. Afterwards, Wolfie would promise to be kinder. But his promises didn't last after he went to school the next day.

Pearl seethed, "I would like to put Wolfie down one of these days."

Isaac declared, "If I have a chance, I'd like him to be afraid of me."

Giselle shook her head. "I don't know if I want to treat Wolfie like that."

Pearl pointed out, "C'mon, he deserves a taste of his own medicine."

Isaac nodded. "Yeah, that bully needs to learn what it's like to be us."

Giselle limped. "That may be true, but I don't think being nasty to him solves everything."

Even though they disagreed with her, Pearl and Isaac knew Giselle was right. However, thoughts of

Wolfie's mistreatment of them burned within the two siblings into fury.

SEVERAL YEARS LATER, Wolfie wandered. At every step into the snow and against the cold wind, he shivered a bit more. The outdoor Christmas decorations didn't lift his spirits. His thin and torn clothes didn't do much to keep him warm. He brushed away snow from his ears and nose.

"Ooooh, I'm c-c-c-cold. I've got t-t-to find a place to s-s-s-stay."

He came upon a huge white mansion. The semi-circular driveway had been shovelled.

"I h-h-h-heard this is where P-p-pearl P-p-p-pig lives nowadays."

He trudged to the front door and rang the doorbell. A rather stiff jackrabbit in a butler's uniform opened the door.

"I'm sorry, sir," declared the butler coldly. "The Madam doesn't want to buy whatever you are selling."

"P-p-please, sir. I just w-w-w-want to talk to P-p-p-pearl. I'm an old sc-sc-schoolmate of hers."

"Your name is?"

"W-w-wolfie."

"One moment, sir."

The butler closed the door, leaving Wolfie shivering faster in the cold. Within a moment, the door was reopened. Pearl appeared in a silky long housecoat over beautiful gown and an angry scowl.

"Hi, P-p-pearl. N-n-n-nice place."

"What do you want?!" Her voice nearly blew him back onto the street.

"Pl-pl-please, Pearl. I know we're n-n-never friends when we w-w-w-were little and I'm tr-tr-truly sorry for all the trouble I have c-c-c-caused on you and your siblings. C-c-c-could you please sp-sp-spare me some clothes and s-s-s-some warm food?"

Pearl stared at Wolfie. "Do you remember the times when you dirtied my clothes with mud?!"

Wolfie nodded.

She demanded, "ANSWER ME!"

Wolfie stammered, "Y-y-yes, I d-d-d-do."

"Do you remember the times when you stole my stuff and returned them?"

"Y-y-yes, I d-d-d-do."

"Do you remember your famous last words? 'You'll never be as great as I'm going to be! Some day I'm going to be famous and everyone will look up to me.'"

"Y-y-yes."

Pearl smirked. "Well, it seems that I'm greater than you are! My husband and I are the financial backbone of this town. We have connections with important people across the country and around the world. This town can't prosper without us. And look at you, a washed-out wanna-be rockstar. I'll bet you have nothing in your bank account. How great are you? Here you are, asking for a morsel of food and a change of clothes."

"H-h-h-how about hiring m-m-m-me as one of your s-s-s-servants?"

Pearl picked him up by his shirt collar and brought his head very close to hers. "I don't recall you being helpful to any of our teachers. In fact, they always sent you to the principal's office because you refused to help clean up. Or you made a mess of someone else's effort. Besides, you're not worthy to take one step into my house." She flung him across the street. "And don't come back here again!"

She slammed the door. "I need to wash my hands. I just got rid of the worst piece of trash."

Wolfie landed into a large garbage bin. He slowly got to his feet, brushed off the paper waste and banana peels, and slowly climbed out the bin. After a few stumbling moves he, continued his journey around town.

AS THE DAY DARKENED into night, Wolfie wandered through a large park. Several screaming drunks scared him. He walked quickly past any small group of thugs before they could question his presence. As he walked on, he wasn't aware that someone was watching him.

He was passing by an apartment building when someone seized him by his tail.

"Yeow!"

"Come on," sneered a big fat tailless cat in a pin-striped suit. His hat almost completely covered his eyes.

The cat hoisted Wolfie over his right shoulder. "The big boss wants to see ya."

"The big boss? Who? Who? Who?"

"Shut up and stop acting like an owl."

The cat stepped up the stairs loudly. Wolfie's head and chest bounced at each step. His head banged upon the doorway as they stepped into the apartment.

Wolfie was very much in a daze when the feline henchman dropped him on the floor. The first thing Wolfie sensed was a nauseating stench of cigar smoke. Shaking his head, Wolfie's eyes focussed at a very fat pig in a white shirt and black tie and pants who was sitting on a very old sofa chair in a corner.

Wolfie asked, "Isaac, is that you?"

Isaac removed his cigar and blew out. The smell caused Wolfie to cough. Isaac snickered as he put his cigar back into his mouth.

"I noticed you at the park, so I sent my pal Maxx to get you. Tell me, Wolfie. What are you doing in my neighbourhood?"

Wolfie stood up. "Well, uh, you see, Isaac, I—"

Isaac sneered at him. "Do you remember those times when you tied my tail to a pole before those races and relays started?"

Wolfie nodded. "Yes, I do. But I just—"

"Do you remember the times when you forced some of us kids to write those sentences over and over again, promising our teachers to behave better? Those tasks were meant for you to do."

Wolfie's knees knocked against each other in fright. "Yes, I do."

"Do you remember your favourite last words? 'You'll never be as great as I'm going to be! Some day I'm going to be famous and everyone will look up to me.'"

"Yes, I do, Isaac."

Isaac laughed. "Well, look at me. I'm very important to everyone who lives in this apartment and this neighbourhood. As long they don't cause trouble to me and Maxx, we won't hassle them too much. Sometimes they ask me some favours and we make sure they repay me promptly. Now look at you. Every time when you tried to form a rock band, it broke up within months. Why? Because you wanted to hog the spotlight and never look out for the needs of your band mates. You lost their respect because you never respected them. Now you have no one to look up to for friendship. All because you only know how to bully, not how to befriend."

Wolfie couldn't stand the guilt any longer. "Please, Isaac. I know we were never friends when we were little and I'm truly sorry for all the trouble I have caused you and your siblings. Could you please let me stay here for a few days?"

Isaac tapped on the coffee table. Maxx reached for a folded paper and handed it to Wolfie.

Isaac explained, "I figure you need a place to stay but have no money. So I drew up a contract. Read it. All I need you to do is a little work in this building, plus, uhhhhh, something which I want you to do before living here."

Unfolding the paper, Wolfie scanned through the contract. His eyes widened in disbelief at the very thing Isaac wanted him to do.

"I have to write 'I will respect, serve and obey Master Isaac Pig for the rest of my life'? Five thousand times?"

The pig grinned. "It's about the equivalent of how many sentences we kids wrote for you. Now what does the contract say if you cause trouble?"

"Maxx will swing me around by my tail for one minute."

"It's for you to remind yourself who is boss around here."

Tossing the contract, Wolfie left the apartment in a panicky state. "I'm out of here!"

He sped out the room.

Maxx demanded, "Hey! Come back here!"

Isaac assured, "Let him go, Maxx. We don't need that worthless good-for-nothing anyway."

As he hurried out of the apartment building, Wolfie didn't see a patch of ice on the sidewalk. As he slipped, he tumbled uncontrollably.

"WHOAAAAAAAAAAAAAAAA!"

Before he knew what was going on, he rolled himself into a giant snowball into the downtown area. All shocked shoppers either stepped back or hurried out of the way. Cars and buses braked as safely as possible without crashing into each other. The snowball smashed into a three-storey building. Wolfie slid down the wall and laid flat on his back.

"Oooooooooooh," he groaned as he slipped into unconsciousness.

"WOLFIE? Wolfie, are you all right?" asked a gentle voice.

When he woke up, it took a few seconds for Wolfie's eyes to readjust from a blurry vision. He found himself lying on a bed in a small room with a small lamp on a nightstand. He felt a heating pad under his back. He lifted an icepack from his forehead. He touched the bandage around his nose. He found himself wearing a clean long-sleeved shirt and brand new jeans.

He bolted upward when he noticed a pig with a cane and an artificial hind leg sitting at his bedside. "Giselle, is that you?"

She gave him a hug. "It's good to see you again."

He hadn't expected her pleasant greeting. "Huh? What? Where am I? The last thing I remember was smashing into a wall."

"You did. You crashed into this homeless shelter; I'm the director. When I heard a noise outside, I found you lying on the sidewalk. I had you brought in here and bandaged. We changed you into these clothes and threw away the ones you were wearing. I waited by your side until you woke up. This is going to be your room. Stay here as long as you want."

Giselle heard Wolfie's stomach growling. "Oh, dear. You're starving. I hate to think when the last time you had a decent meal was. Can you get up and walk?"

He slowly stood up. He wobbled until he regained his balance. "I think so."

She took his paw. "Come, I'll show you to the dining hall."

She led him downstairs to a very spacious hall and guided him to the lengthy buffet table. Soft Christmas music played from a small stereo. After making his choices, Wolfie sat at one of the tables and started to eat.

Wolfie had expected Giselle to torture his conscience the way her siblings did. However, he was overwhelmed by the warm atmosphere. Many of the shelter staff and homeless guests made small talk with him and became fast friends.

A homeless raccoon gave him an extra guitar and the two played songs which, by coincidence, both knew. Everyone enjoyed their performance. For the first time in his life, Wolfie felt loved and accepted.

However, there was one thing which puzzled him very much.

Later, Wolfie headed upstairs to his room with his new possession. Giselle came out of her office.

"See you in the morning, Wolfie," she bade.

Wolfie called, "Hold it, Giselle. I want to ask you something."

"Sure."

They walked into the empty lounge and sat on the green couch.

"What is it, Wolfie?"

"Giselle, how come you're different from Pearl and Isaac? I went to see them today, but they rejected me. Yet you acted as if we've been friends for a very long time, even though I have never acted like one."

Giselle thought for a moment. "Let me ask you a few questions."

He took a deep breath. "I'm listening."

"Do you remember the times when you tripped my cane, causing me to lose my balance and fall?"

He lowered his head in despair. "Yes, I do."

She gently tilted his head up. "Do you remember the times when you said mean things to us kids when you were supposed to be encouraging?"

He nodded.

"Do you remember your favourite last words? 'You'll never be as great as I'm going to be! Some day I'm going to be famous and everyone will look up to me."

A tear ran down his face. "Yes, I do."

She wiped his tear away. "Let me tell you this: I don't think much about what you have done. Rather, I have been concerned about you."

Wolfie was surprised. "Why is that?"

"Because I have already forgiven you a long time ago. I figured out your true nature. Ever since you were little, you wanted attention. But you didn't get much of it from your parents because they were so busy with their work and their own interests. So, in order for them to notice you more, you decided to be mean to us. Their reactions at every call from the principal might not have given you words of praise, but all you wanted from your parents was attention."

She paused. "As for not being 'as great as I'm going to be,' of course we won't be as great as you wanted yourself to be. That's because we each have different talents and limitations. For me, even though I had my leg amputated a few years ago and now need my cane to get around, that won't stop me from caring for others. You may not turn out to be famous, but everyone enjoyed your music with your new friend today. Your music makes everyone happy. I heard they want you two to perform tomorrow." Giselle sighed. "It's too bad my siblings don't think the same way about you as I do. Pearl wants nothing to do with you. Isaac wants revenge. As long they continue to think about you like that, they'll never be at peace. That's why I chose to forgive you. Forgiveness bears peace and love, not an endless grudge."

Wolfie sighed deeply. "This is new stuff to me. I'm overwhelmed. Today I learned what it's like to have friends. But I still have a little feeling there may be others who still want to get back at me because I was a bad wolf."

Giselle touched his shoulder. "Let me ask you one more question: While you were making friends during dinner, do you feel that someone has a reason to hate you?"

Wolfie shook his head. "No, not one."

She smiled. "Neither do I. Go to bed now and be bad no more. Merry Christmas."

> *"Do not do wrong to repay a wrong, and*
> *do not insult to repay an insult. But*
> *repay with a blessing, because you*
> *yourselves were called to do this so that*
> *you might receive a blessing."*

—1 Peter 3:9 (NCV)

One More

"HEY, GLAD you can make it," greeted Zachary as he welcomed his employees into an enormous banquet hall. The walls and tables were decked with Christmas decorations. Servers in stiff uniforms moved around the room, serving finger foods and beverages while others worked at setting the tables. Strains of traditional Christmas music could be heard coming from the small orchestra in one corner of the room. A cash bar served drinks. Between the bar and the band stood a Christmas tree with a large basket of gifts underneath it.

Zachary watched his employees enjoying themselves. They munched and talked to one another. Some men talked to the bartenders. A few brave couples danced as the orchestra played. Occasionally, an employee grabbed the microphone and lightened up the mood with a stand-up comedian act.

Zachary sat with his assistant Xaviera at the reception table. "It looks like everyone showed up. The room is almost filled to the max."

She looked at her clipboard. "Not everyone, Zack. There are about five who have yet to show up."

He chuckled as he got up. "Great. In every party, there has to be a few slowpokes. We'll start the dinner in forty-five minutes, Xaviera, so do come in. I'm sure the latecomers will find their way."

After the delightful meal, Zachary distributed gifts to his employees. He stood near the Christmas tree. Whenever he called out a name, the staff member would hurry to him, take the gift, and thank him. This went on until the boss came upon the last gift.

"Henry Dublet!"

Silence hung throughout the room. No footsteps were heard coming towards Zachary. Only Zachary scanned the room to see where Henry was.

Zachary called, "Henry Dublet! Henry, where are you?"

Xaviera hurried to his side. "He's the only one who hasn't shown up. I tried calling his home and cell, but no answer."

He sighed, "I was afraid this was going to happen."

Leon declared, "Just save the gift for him until Monday and let's continue with the festivities!"

Zachary sensed a disturbing feeling amongst his staff. "Everyone assumed Henry wouldn't be here?"

Leon ranted, "You bet, we did. He's become someone who we don't know. About a month ago, I was going around my usual bit, collecting money for lottery tickets. When I came upon him, he told me he didn't want to participate anymore. I was surprised, because he used to be the most enthusiastic person in the group. I tried to assure him that we're going to win someday. I also reminded him of that boat he has been wanting to get. He told me there wouldn't be a boat for him. I told him there are other things money can buy. He then pushed me against a wall and looked me straight in the eye. He muttered at me to find someone else to 'play the game.'"

Xaviera remarked, "You should have respected his wish not to be included in the lottery pool anymore."

Vanessa spoke up, "How about this? Did you hear him screaming at me four weeks ago? I simply pointed out an error and he scolded me for being critical. He apologized to me and corrected the mistake. But that wasn't the first time he yelled at me for something that is so small."

Arnold added, "The last time some of us guys went out to lunch with him, he ordered an appetizer and water. We teased him for being cheap. I joked that he'd be hungry for the rest of the day. He got up, paid enough money to give our server twice the tip, and left. We didn't mean to embarrass him, but he didn't have to take it personally."

Xaviera kindly pointed out, "I do find it a bit hard to talk to him. It is almost as if he doesn't want to talk to anyone. Besides, no one has seen him around lately."

Zachary explained, "That's because he now works from 8:00 p.m. to 4:00 a.m. On Fridays, he wanted everything e-mailed to his home computer."

Like everyone else, Leon was surprised to hear it. "What? Why so late?"

"He didn't think anyone would want him around, due to his unpredictable outbursts and mood swings. Two weeks ago, he asked me to change his work schedule. I asked him if there was anything bothering him. He wouldn't give details. I can tell that he went through something horrible enough to change him from being a cheerful guy who always says good morning with the biggest smile to a very depressed, reclusive soul. He's beginning to look gaunt, as if he hasn't been eating enough."

Vanessa commented, "Poor guy. If only we knew what he's going through—"

Leon interrupted, "Like I said, give him the gift on Monday. We'll apologize to him when we see him. C'mon, let's get on with the night."

Xaviera scolded, "How can you think about having fun when there is a coworker moping somewhere out there? He's part of us; we're not a complete team without him."

Zachary turned to his assistant. "Xaviera, what day is it today?"

"Friday."

Everyone watched as their boss hurried towards the entrance of the hall. Arnold called, "Where are you going?"

"Out to look for Henry."

Leon suggested, "Check out every bar."

Vanessa pointed out, "He doesn't like alcohol and bars. Everyone knows that."

Leon shrugged. "He may have change his habits if he is truly that depressed."

She jabbed her elbow into his stomach. He let out a loud yelp.

Zachary ordered, "Xaviera, tell the kitchen staff to warm the remaining food. Nobody leaves here until I bring back Henry."

For the next hour, Zachary wandered downtown. He walked through alleys where drunks and the homeless loitered. He kept his eyes and ears alert. A few times, he mistook strangers for Henry.

A thought circled around in his mind. Why did he insist on working at home on Fridays?

As Zachary passed by a community centre, he heard a voice through a window that stood ajar.

"I'm sorry I waited for a long time to open up."

Zachary stopped. "Henry?"

He headed into the community centre. Peering into an opened room, he saw thirteen people sitting on chairs in a circle. He recognized Henry's attire—white shirt, blue jacket and pants with grey patches all over, and a baseball cap.

"My life spiralled out of control," spoke Henry. "A little more than a month ago, my doctor told me I have cancer. He told me that if I had surgery, I would have a better chance of surviving. I was planning to ask my boss about my health insurance when I was hit by another bombshell. My wife walked out of my life. She said she couldn't see herself taking care of a sick man. She found someone else more flawless than me. My self-esteem crashed like glass smashed against a concrete floor. I gave up my dream of owning a boat to save for the operation. I didn't eat much. My emotions went berserk. I found myself yelling at my coworkers. My good boss let me work a different shift so I wouldn't have as much contact with people. I also work at home on Fridays so that I can be with you guys on time. I like working alone so no one will see me cry."

The counsellor, the blonde who sat beside Henry, placed her hand on his shoulder. "It's good for you to share your burden with us. You have to tell everything to your colleagues. I'm sure they'll be very understanding. You don't have to work out your sadness and struggles alone."

All heads nodded in agreement.

Henry sighed. "I'm very grateful to be here and getting to know you guys. Your stories have been an inspiration to me to press on living, even at times when I feel like hiding in the dark."

One of attendees declared, "You don't have to be afraid of cancer. Cancer can be beaten."

The counsellor glanced at her watch. "I'm sorry, folks, but we only have enough time for refreshments. Please keep in touch with one another. I'll see you again next week."

Everyone stood up. Some took turns embracing Henry and uttering a few encouraging words.

"Be strong, brother."

"Don't be afraid. Everything will be all right."

"Take good care of yourself."

Henry was about to head to the refreshment table when Zachary called, "Henry."

Astonished, Henry turned to see his employer. "Zack, how long have you been here?"

"Long enough to hear your story."

Henry looked at Zachary's clothes. "How's the party?"

"It went well, except for one thing."

"What's that?"

"It's not the same without you. In fact, it won't continue until you join us."

Henry looked at his clothes. "I'm not even dressed to party."

"It doesn't matter. You look fine. All we want is you."

Henry hesitated. "I don't know, Zack. Y'know, everyone hates me and I don't blame them."

"As soon you explain everything about your cancer, I'm sure a lot will be very sympathetic. We'll help you deal with your cancer. I'll do everything I can to make sure the insurance covers the operation."

Henry was flabbergasted. "You're sure?"

"We'll do whatever we can to help you stay alive. Besides, you will always be a part of the company. We want you back."

Zachary put his arm around him. "We still have more than enough to help you get your strength back. C'mon, let's go back to the party."

*"Do all that you can to live in peace
with everyone."*

—Romans 12:18 (NLT)

Santa's Deliverance

"GOOD MORNING, Santa Delivers," greeted Barney over the phone. In his warehouse office, he received phone calls from people who requested gifts for children either living in impoverished neighbourhoods or staying in hospitals. Two weeks before Christmas, he would dress up as Santa Claus and deliver the requests.

A child's voice spoke, "Hello. My name is Sarah and I want you to give something to my friend in the hospital."

Barney smiled as he grabbed a pad and pen. "Certainly. What's your friend's name?"

"Qucisha."

"What hospital is she staying in?"

"Judah Memorial Hospital."

"What room is she in?"

"C69. Children's Ward."

"And what does Queisha want for Christmas? A doll?"

"No."

"A crossword book or some games?"

"No."

"How about chocolate bars?"

"No."

Barney chuckled, "Okay, I give up. What does she wants?"

"A hug."

Barney jumped in his seat. "A hug? Don't her mommy and daddy give her hugs everyday?"

"They died three years ago. She has been in a few foster homes, but no one wants to adopt her. She has no friends but me to visit her. No one else from school even dared to come close to her. Now she'd like a hug from Santa."

"Why does she want a hug?"

"She wants to prove that you can't get AIDS from hugging someone who has it."

Barney's jaw dropped in disbelief. "AIDS? Queisha has AIDS?"

"It's not her fault and neither was it her parents'. Her mommy got a bad blood transfusion a year before Queisha was born. When the children's home requested a blood test on her, doctors discovered she has AIDS."

Barney tried to remain composed. "Um, listen, honey. I'll try to make a special stop to see her when I go to the hospital."

"I hope you will soon because she may die one day. She has hopes that you'll be there to see here before Christmas."

"All right, I will. Thank you for your call, Sarah."

"Thank you very much, Santa. Bye."

"Bye."

As soon he hung up, Barney breathed in exhaustion. "A child with AIDS."

His assistant Yoko stepped into his office. "I was about to come into your office when I heard your side of the conversation. I hope you're going to fulfill that girl's wish."

In desperation, he asked, "What am I supposed to do?"

"If you don't make that visit, not only are you going to dash that sick girl's wish to pieces, but also her friend's trust in your effort to keep your promise. That will have a ripple effect if this spreads to their friends and Santa's reputation as a whole will be at stake. That will throw our charity work into chaos."

"I have never met anyone with AIDS. I don't know how to deal with them."

"You don't believe that you can get AIDS through hugging, do you?"

Barney shrugged. "Yes. I mean no. I mean, yes, I understand that you don't get AIDS from hugging, talking, or whatever with someone who has it. It's just . . . well, I don't like to see a child dying on Christmas. It scares me to know that not all children will get to see everything in his or her short life."

Yoko studied Barney's face. "You're still thinking about Tabitha, aren't you?"

He sighed, "I miss Tabitha, my daughter. That little girl's story about her friend's parents sounded very similar to my own story. My first impression of Tabitha's fiancé Nolan was wonderful. He was a good man. Then, I heard a news story about a man who was wanted by the police for murder. His description fit Nolan exactly. I tried to warn her, but Tabitha assured me that Nolan was nowhere near to those crime scenes. As I heard more news about the elusive killer, I acted more paranoid. I hired a private investigator to follow Nolan; he also found nothing unusual about him. I warned friends. Tabitha and Nolan were getting frustrated of my surveillance. Finally they had enough and left town. When the real killer was caught, I was dumbfounded. Nolan had been innocent all along. It took a long time for my neighbours to trust me again. For almost seven years, I have wanted to make up with them but I have no way of doing so. I created this charity to deal with my loss."

Yoko thought for a moment. "Even though you have helped children have a memorable Christmas, it still hasn't given you closure with your own family."

Barney shook his head. "No, I don't even feel at peace."

"Where is Queisha staying?"

"The Children's Ward at Judah Memorial Hospital."

"Good timing."

"Why?"

"I was about to remind you that today we're to go there and give gifts to the sick kids. This is a wonderful opportunity to see the little girl."

He stared at her in disbelief. "Today? Are you sure?"

Yoko nodded. "This can be the very day Queisha sees Santa."

"Ho! Ho! Ho! Merry Christmas, boys and girls!" proclaimed Barney in his Santa suit, white beard, and wig as he handed gifts to children in their hospital beds in a large room. Behind him, Yoko, dressed as a yellow and green elf, passed him the presents from a huge sack. All the young patients laughed with glee as they opened their gifts.

"Wow! A handheld video game!" exclaimed one boy.

"A set of toy soldiers!" declared another one.

"A 'Young Actress' make-up set," proclaimed a girl.

"An artist's case with markers, crayons, papers, and other stuff!" laughed another girl.

"Thank you, Santa!" shouted the children.

"Hope you have a wonderful New Year! Get well!" bade Barney as he and Yoko left the room.

A supervising doctor, Kirk, met the pair. "On behalf of the hospital, I want to thank you for your yearly visit to the children."

Barney smiled. "It's always been our pleasure, Kirk."

Yoko added. "We love to see all the children happy at this time of the year."

There was a pause until Yoko nudged Barney with her elbow. Trying to conceal his reluctance, Barney asked, "Kirk, is there a little girl with AIDS by the name of Quiesha? We received a call from a friend of hers."

Kirk sighed, "Oh, yes. Quiesha. Poor girl. She couldn't come to be with the other kids."

Yoko asked, "Why? The other children don't want to be with her."

"No, this morning she had a high fever. By the time we stabilized her, you guys were already here. Daily she's been waiting for a visit from Santa to give her a hug. That's all she asks for Christmas."

Barney hesitantly nodded. "We would like to see her now. After all, I did promise her friend to come and see her."

Kirk grinned. "Okay, this way."

The doctor led Barney and Yoko to a room at the very end of the hall. Knocking on the door lightly, Kirk instructed, "Stay here for a moment. I'm going in there to check whether she's awake."

Kirk entered the room and closed the door behind him. Barney and Yoko leaned against the wall. He glared at her in scorn. "You have to drag me here."

"Do I have to remind you who you're supposed to be?"

Kirk opened the door. "Okay, you can come in now. She's a little tired, but she's well enough for some company. I can only give you ten minutes."

Yoko said, "Thanks, Doctor."

As Barney and Yoko entered the room, Quiesha sat up smiling. The only noticeable possession was a framed photo of a man, woman, and infant on a night table next to her bed.

The child stretched out her arms. "Santa Claus!"

Barney wrapped his arms around her. "Ho! Ho! Ho! Merry Christmas, Quiesha."

He was hoping for a brief hug, but she embraced him longer than he anticipated. Yoko tried to hide her giggles. After a few moments, Quiesha released her hold.

Straightening himself up, Barney remarked, "My, you're such an experienced hugger, Quiesha."

"I've been waiting for you everyday. Now my Christmas wish has come true."

"How are you feeling?" asked Yoko.

"I was sick this morning. But when you're here, I feel a lot better. I know now that I will have a happy Christmas."

Yoko picked up the photo. "This looks like a happy family."

"That's my daddy, mommy, and me when I was a baby. They died of AIDS after I turned three. That picture was taken six years ago. Now I'm dying of AIDS."

After a mere glance at the photo, Barney did a double-take. Seizing the photo, he took a closer look.

Yoko noticed his surprised look. "Barney," she whispered, "what is it?"

"It's Tabitha and Nolan," he responded in a hushed whisper.

Yoko gasped. "Are you sure?"

"I'm positive. If Quiesha is Tabitha and Nolan's daughter . . ."

"We have found your granddaughter."

Barney shook his head. "All these years and I missed my chance to see them forever."

Yoko squeezed his shoulder. "I think you can make up that chance through their daughter."

Quiesha became curious. "Is something wrong, Santa?"

Barney gently placed the photo back onto the night table. "We're just stunned at how wonderful your parents looked. Tell me this: do you have any relatives?"

"I have a grandpa and I've seen a few photos of him. But I never met him."

Yoko asked, "How did your parents feel about your grandpa?"

"I think they loved him and they hoped that he will see me one day."

Barney asked, "Do you want to see your grandpa?"

Quiesha bent her knees and wrapped her arms around her legs. "Yeah, but I don't know how. I don't know where he lives. That's why I want a hug from you, Santa, for Christmas. I know I will get it for sure. But my grandpa, I don't even know if he'll love me, because I'm sick."

Barney laid his hand upon her shoulder. "Quiesha, do you want to believe that your grandpa loves you regardless of whether you're sick or not?"

"Yeah. Would you know?"

"I'm sure if he finds you here, your grandpa will love you."

Quiesha's eyes brightened. "You think so?"

"If you believe what I say, I'm sure that's another Christmas wish that will come true."

The child gave him another hug. This time, he accepted it graciously. A tear made its way down his face.

Reaching into the sack, Yoko pulled out a teddy bear with a red ribbon tied around its waist. "Quiesha, we know that you just want hugs for Christmas, but let us give this to you. At least, you won't be lonely in this room."

The girl took it. "Thank you very much."

Barney waved. "We have to be going. Merry Christmas, Quiesha."

"Merry Christmas, Santa. Thank you."

After they left the room, Kirk hurried towards them. "I was on my way to remind you that you have five minutes left."

Barney asked, "Is she allowed any more visitors?"

The doctor thought for a moment. "I believe so."

Barney slapped Kirk on the back. "Good."

Barney and Yoko stopped outside the men's washroom. "Yoko, could you please wait here while I get out of this costume? Afterwards, you can take my outfit and whatever's left in the van back to the warehouse and go home for the rest of the day."

She nodded. "I'm happy for you."

He sniffed. "I haven't felt at peace like this for a long time."

After Barney disappeared into the men's room, Kirk approached Yoko. "What was that all about?"

"Quiesha has given him the very thing he has been wanting for a long time."

"That is?"

"Reaffirmation of family."

"Bear with each other and forgive
whatever grievances you may have
against one another. Forgive as the Lord
forgave you. And over all these virtues
put on love, which binds them all
together in perfect unity."

—Colossians 3:13–14 (NIV)

2008

THIS STORY WAS to be looked upon as an aftermath to the story "Goldilocks and the Three Bears." I added a hint of my favourite non-competitive reality show, "Extreme Makeover: Home Edition," with this thought: what if there was a needy family whose member was so stubborn and bitter that the design team couldn't approach them in their usual manner? This story focussed on restoring one's peace from prejudice. One cannot see another's true character without resolving his or her prejudice or obscured perception.

Makeover for the Heart

THERE WAS a family of bears who lived in a house at the edge of the woods. Lately, they hadn't dwelled in comfort and the father wasn't happy. He paced heavily in the living room.

"Water's overflowed in the washer! Air conditioner conked out! The plaster on the bathroom ceiling is cracking! I can't afford to buy a heater and winter's coming soon! I tried to fix the front door, but it kept falling off the hinges! If it weren't for that little human with yellow hair, these problems wouldn't happen! Humans! You can't trust them! You can never like them!"

His wife placed her paw on his shoulder. "Now, Ken. The little human didn't know she's not supposed to go into someone's house without permission. Besides, that was three years ago. Our house problems only started three months ago."

But Ken wouldn't still his mouth. "Three years! Three months! Who cares about time, Urika? Sooner or later, this house will fall apart and we'll have nowhere else to go! It's too expensive to fix everything and save for our son's education! The dam isn't making profit lately, and there hasn't been enough fish! We may not be able to afford anything for the winter! Why are we cursed? What did that human bring in here?"

Steaming in fury, he headed upstairs.

Their son was playing with his toys nearby. "Mama?"

She walked over to him. "Yes, Otis?"

"Are we living like this because of humans?"

She chuckled, "No, your Papa got this house long before we became a family. Now everything seems to become old and doesn't work the way it should."

"Why is Papa blaming humans?"

"When he's angry, he needs someone to blame. I guess he can't forget that day when that little girl came here and ate our breakfast, tried our chairs, and slept in our bedroom. Whenever I look back on that day, I pitied that young human's lack of proper courtesy. That kept me in good perspective and from unneeded anger."

"She broke my chair, but Papa built me a new one. I'm okay with that."

She nodded. "Your kind heart has been your blessing. You never uttered a harsh word."

She sighed. "If only your Papa could learn a thing or two from you. He's been grumbling about her ever since that incident."

"I don't recall him being pleasant."

"He did have a few joyful times, but those did not outshine his angry years. I kept telling him he's been grumbling in his sleep lately."

"When will Papa be happy again?"

"The sooner the better."

A FEW MONTHS later, the Bear family was relaxing in their family room. Ken was reading the newspaper. Urika was knitting a cap. Otis was playing with his cars. The lights flickered, and then went out.

"Oh dear," said Urika.

Ken's temper flared. "And it's that little human again!"

Otis asked, "Papa, how come you keep saying it's her fault? She may have nothing to do with it."

"I suppose you think there's another explanation!"

His wife asked, "Dear, did you remember to pay the electricity bill?"

He sneered, "What do you mean by that?"

Her voice became firmer. "Did you or did you not?"

"I must have. I don't see it on my desk!"

Taking a flashlight from the table next to her, Urika left the room. She came back moments later with an envelope in her hand. She gave it to her husband and shone the flashlight at it.

She asked, "What does the front of the envelope say?"

Ken sheepishly answered, "Forest Glen Electricity Company."

"I remember putting it there about six weeks ago. You still haven't opened it."

Otis asked, "Now do you believe it's not the little human's fault?"

He grumbled as he trudged out the room. His wife and son could hear him bumping into objects.

"Urika, bring that flashlight to me, would you?"

"I'm coming."

A FEW WEEKS later, they heard a loud racket of hammering, sawing, and large machines moving about. They headed to the living room window.

"Look, Mama and Papa. They're building a new house across from us."

Urika remarked, "New neighbours. How wonderful."

Ken grumbled, "That family will have things better than we have."

She scolded, "Ken, don't talk like that, especially in front of our son."

"Look at our home, Urika! It's falling apart and I can't keep up with the repairs! Those humans will be showing off their possessions endlessly! It will be a headache to all of us to hear those stories over and over again!"

Otis asked, "How do you know humans will be moving into that house, Papa?"

"Only humans can afford houses that size!"

Urika scolded, "Ken, enough of that ungrateful talk. Be thankful for the goodness you have."

"Oh yeah? Like, what?"

She embraced him. "You have us."

Otis hugged him.

Ken dared not argue, but slowly he wrapped one arm around his wife and, with his other hand, patted his son's head.

MONTHS LATER, Urika was washing the dishes when she heard the banging of the front door, followed by her husband's raging anger. Otis hurried into the kitchen and held her.

"Otis, what's wrong? I thought Papa was playing catch with you."

"We were until he noticed someone taking pictures of us."

She thought for a moment. "You know, I thought I noticed some strange flashes after you two left."

"Plus the front door came off after he slammed it."

She shook her head. "Oh, dear."

Drying her hands with her apron, she hurried to her enraged husband, who was jumping on the door. Her son followed closely behind her.

"This house is cursed! My family is cursed! If it weren't for that little human, we'd be at peace!"

"Dear—"

"I want to live the way we used to! Without any kind of intrusions from these humans!"

Urika had enough of his complaints. "Then may I make a suggestion?"

He stopped jumping. "What?!"

"Go and live outside."

Ken was infuriated. "What kind of a suggestion is that? It would be as bad as living here!"

"I know, but Otis and I will be living in peace without your constant dissatisfaction. Besides, most bears roam in the great outdoors."

"But I don't want to live outside! This is my home!"

"Then stop acting like a child with an endless temper tantrum. Otis and I don't want to hear another raging growl from you. If you need to blow your top, go outside and far away, so we won't hear you. And come back when you're done. Keep in mind that winter is coming. But then again, the chills should help you cool down. Right now I suggest you fix the front door."

Before Ken could utter another word, Urika and Otis hurried back to the kitchen. He stepped off the door and looked at it.

"They don't believe in curses," he mumbled. "They don't believe in me."

IN EARLY DECEMBER, when snow covered the forest, Urika cuddled Otis on her lap on a comfortable sofa chair. She wrapped a thick quilt around them. She rocked her body. Despite this, they were disturbed by the sounds of stomping above them.

"Papa is still unhappy, isn't he, Mama?"

She shook her head and looked at the fallen Christmas tree in front of them. "I don't feel like asking him to go outside and cool off. Also, his stomping made our Christmas tree fall for the tenth time this week."

"At least he isn't complaining aloud."

There was a knock on the front door. Putting Otis on the floor, Urika hurried over, removed the duct tape, and lifted the door aside. At the doorway stood a woman in a long hooded coat and a hard helmet.

"Hello," greeted Urika, "may I help you?

"Hello, Mrs. Bear. My name is Charity. I'm actually here to help you and your family."

"Oh? In what way?

"Just come out and follow me. All of you, please. I have something to show you."

Urika turned to her cub. "Go and get our coats, please."

As Otis headed to the main closet, Ken came down. He bellowed, "What's going on? And who—"

Urika hurried to him. "Not another word. Get your coat from Otis. This lady is going to show us something."

"Why do you—"

She slapped her hand onto his mouth. "I said not another word. Just keep an open mind and follow us."

They trudged through the thick snow. Urika hoped the visitor didn't hear Ken's grumbling. Whenever she heard him muttering too loud, she poked his stomach with her elbow.

They arrived at the newly built house. Ken sneered, "So, this is what you're going to show us? That's fine. Goodbye."

As Ken turned to leave, Urika pulled him back. "Don't be rude. Charity's not done yet."

Charity opened the door. "Would you like to come in and look around?"

Urika dragged her husband in. "We'd love to."

The family explored the house. All the furniture and appliance appeared to shine under the skylight and hanging lamps. The child's bedroom seemed to be overstuffed and organized with toys, books and clothes. The master bedroom was decorated simply beautifully; the en suite bathroom included a Jacuzzi bathtub. Every room displayed photographs of the family.

"Isn't this house beautiful, Ken?"

When she didn't get a response, Urika knew her husband was still fuming.

"Ken, I said, isn't this house beautiful?"

"Yes, dear."

Otis remarked, "This is so cool."

Ken was about to scold his son when Urika nudged him to keep quiet. He rolled up his eyes.

They regrouped in the living room. Charity asked, "Well, what do you think?"

Before Urika could reply, Ken's impatience exploded. "How dare you spy on my family! You better not send those photos to the tabloids or any circus master!"

His wife scolded, "Ken, hold your tongue! Where are your manners?"

"Didn't you count how many pictures of us there are in this house of hers?"

"Are you dumb? This is not meant to be her house!"

"Whose house is it going to be?"

She touched his arm. "Ours."

Ken's fury seemed to disappear. "Ours?"

Otis approached the woman. "Ours?"

She patted his head. "It's all yours and everything has been paid for. Electricity, heating, phone, and Internet have also been taken care for the next five years. I also set aside an abundant education fund for your son."

Otis said, "Thanks."

Charity added, "I also have plenty of money for Mr. Bear to start his own fish business. There's a huge pond not too far from the back of the house with an abundance of fish."

Ken demanded, "How on earth are we going to pay you for all this?"

"This is the Christmas season, isn't it? So, it's my Christmas gift to you all."

Urika asked, "How can you afford all this?"

"My father died earlier this year. My family inherited a huge sum of money and we know we can't use it all for ourselves. So, when we saw your house becoming something beyond repair, we decided to surprise you with the new one we just finished building. I also sent my husband to secretly—as secretly as possible, anyway—take pictures of you. I was hoping these framed photos would add a touch of family into this place. Now our inheritance is down to the amount we're comfortable with."

Ken was still sceptical of Charity's generosity. "Since this is Christmas, is there anything you want?"

Urika whispered, "Ken."

Charity replied, "There is one thing we want from you alone, Mr. Bear."

"Aha! I knew there was a catch!"

His wife scolded, "Dear, don't be rude."

Charity said, "The very thing we would like from you, Mr. Bear, is that you would accept my daughter's apology for the things she did three years ago."

Ken was shocked. "What?"

Charity removed her helmet, revealing her short blond hair. The family was surprised. Their eyes widened at the revelation.

Ken rapidly asked, "You? Your daughter? What?"

Urika clarified his words. "You are the little girl's mother?"

Charity nodded. "Goldilocks—she'd rather be called Goldwyn now—was sorry about everything she did. She came into your house without permission, spoiled your breakfast, damaged your chairs, and messed up your beds."

Otis pointed out, "But ma'am, only my porridge was eaten, my chair was broken, and my bed was slept in."

She nodded. "I know, but you weren't the only one affected. Your mama and papa also were saddened by your loss."

Ken asked, "Why can't she just come here and apologize?"

"She tried, but she couldn't. She was frightened by all the words of accusation and bitterness she heard. From what I can figure out, all those harsh words came from you, Mr. Bear. You may want an apology from my daughter, but those loud complaints of yours barred her from doing so. That's why we had this house built before telling you folks."

Both Urika and Otis glared at him whose head hung low in guilt and shame. Urika pointed out, "Now do you see what your temper has done? Not only did it ruin the girl's opportunity to apologize, but it also made us miss the chance of hearing it. We've been warning you to keep our home peaceful, but it seems you enjoyed making a loud racket everyday. I hope you've learned who really made our home fall apart."

"Yes, dear."

Charity asked, "Would you like to have the opportunity which you've missed several times?"

Ken nodded. "Sure, I'm ready."

The woman walked to the front door and opened it. There stood a young girl in pink winter clothes. Her blond hair fluttered with the wind. She looked fearful at Ken.

Charity beckoned, "It's all right, dear. Come in. No one's going to hurt you."

Goldwyn entered timidly. Her heart pounded as if it were trying to get out her chest. She appeared to be on a verge of tears.

Otis waved at her. "Hello."

She gave a weak smile.

Ken approached her, but she ran and hid behind her mother.

"He's going to yell at me again, Mom!" Goldwyn cried.

"No, he's not, Goldwyn. He has something to say to you, too."

Ken crouched down to Goldwyn's eye-level. "Goldwyn?" She wiped her eyes. "I won't get angry at you," he assured her.

Hesitantly, the girl moved to face him.

Ken said, "I'm sorry for yelling bad things about you."

Goldwyn stammered, "I-I-I've been w-w-w-wanting to say I'm s-s-s-sorry for messing up your house."

He nodded. "I know. I should have been more willing to hear you say that."

He patted her head. "It's all right. All's forgiven."

Goldwyn flung her arms around his neck and burst into tears. He embraced her like a father loving his daughter.

"I forgive you, too," declared Goldwyn.

Ken whispered, "Thank you. Thank you very much."

Otis sniffed, wiping a tear from his right eye. "Oh, Mama. This is wonderful."

Urika nodded. "I know. I can see we're going to have peace in this house."

Charity smiled. "This definitely completes the makeover."

"Let us therefore make every effort to do what leads to peace and to mutual edification."

—Romans 14:19 (NIV)

2009

EARLY IN THE YEAR, I wasn't sure what to write. I had a few ideas, but in the middle of each one, I got stuck and couldn't continue. Then I sensed the background topic should reflect the worldwide theme of financial recession. This story was about a department's team leader who went through extremes to make sure that not only his employees still kept their jobs, but also the less fortunate in his community were being looked after. He did it without much financial outside help. His actions were enough to perk up an unpopular worker's curiosity.

The Scaled-Down

Executive

VADIM LEANED against the department's kitchen counter while he waited for the coffeemaker to complete its first brew.

"Morning. How are you doing?" he greeted every coworker coming to leave their lunches in the fridge.

Let's see, he thought. What do I have for today? Print out last Friday's sales report. Check the department's lottery numbers. Go through all of today's product request applications and check for errors. Hang around the staff lounge to catch any latest news. Type up my daily report. Skim through the newspapers for any games playing tonight. Go online to check for any of the company's upcoming new products. Catch up with my e-mails, if I have time.

He turned to the coffeemaker and poured some coffee into his cup.

Nothing like the first cup of the day, especially in winter.

Vadim had just stepped out of the kitchen when he saw a large black man in a long beige coat entering the department. He was carrying his briefcase.

Uh-oh, it's Jethro, back from his vacation. I'd better head over to my desk.

Vadim headed to his desk, whistling. Those who heard him watched him passing by.

"What's with Vadim?" asked a coworker.

AS JETHRO ENTERED his office, his administrative assistant looked up from her computer.

"Good morning, Jethro. Welcome back."

"Good morning, Halima. How's everyone?"

"Business as usual. The only good news is that no one is laid off. The company's president announced on Friday that nobody will be receiving the pink slip."

Jethro placed his briefcase down. "That's good to hear."

She added, "And that was close. Nearly three weeks ago, everyone was tense over the possibility of losing their jobs. Yet, you knew what to do while you were away. I don't know, but it seems as though you've made a lot of sacrifices to bail everyone out."

"I simply changed my perspective on life and that itself started the ball rolling. And it will continue to roll."

"Everyone is surprised of the unexpected pay increase last Thursday. Even the contract workers are permitted to work for an extra year."

He smiled. "Then I guess no one is afraid of the word 'recession' anymore."

She shook her head. "I still can't believe it. All the financial woes of this company disappeared. It's like someone saved a weak swimmer by using CPR."

"When you work for a company, you have to do whatever it takes to keep it alive. Even if it means extreme personal actions."

"Extreme, indeed. I don't recall any other team managers who do similar deeds to yours."

He looked at his watch. "We better keep on going before the day finishes. As soon I settle myself down, we'll go through today's agenda."

She nodded. "Right. I'm almost finished with the team's monthly report, which I need you to proofread before I can send it to the company's president."

He picked up his briefcase. "Fine, I'll see you shortly."

LATER IN THE DAY, Jethro was working at his laptop when Vadim knocked at his door. In his hand were a few sheets of papers. Jethro beckoned him to enter. Closing the door behind him, Vadim approached him.

"Good morning, Jethro. I know I should wait, but Halima isn't at her desk right now and your door's open." You must have a very nice two-week vacation."

Jethro smiled. "Not exactly a vacation. I had to take care of a lot of things; some are personal. But yes, it's good to be back, so I can continue with my work."

Vadim handed him the papers. "Can you believe this? The profits jumped back up. We got new clients getting our products, especially our new and improved insurance policies. It's like we're getting back to normal."

Jethro glanced at the reports. "Not exactly. Every company, including this one, is watching out for unpredictable changes in the financial world."

"Of course, we have to be very careful with our money."

"Not just careful. We also have to be very considerate with it."

His remark jolted Vadim into curiosity. "What do you mean?"

"You'll see. As you know, there will be a lot of new things happening around here. Remember this for now: It's good to conserve money for a rainy day, but rain or shine, it's also a good thing to commit money for the well-being of others. This also applies to resources and time."

Still confused, Vadim stood up. "Yeah, whatever. I'll see you later."

As Vadim hurried out the office, Halima came in. "What's with him?"

Jethro lightly chuckled, "Oh, we had a little talk. I didn't give him all the details."

"Be glad that you didn't. Yes, he is a good worker, but he also can be a busybody. He usually talks to others to find things to gossip about. A lot of people, including myself, have been very careful of what to say to him without making him feel left out."

"Be patient with him. He may not be comfortable with the new implementations that will happen starting today after hours. He'll learn what's more important not only for the company, but also for all of us individually."

"I hope so. He can be very opinionated on everything."

She turned to leave. "Especially if he were to find out what kind of neighbours you have now."

"Yes, I know."

VADIM PACED in circles by the elevators. Every few seconds, he checked his watch.

What are these elevators trying to do? Waste my break time?

He heard the sound of a stampede behind him. He watched as a group of colleagues, led by Jethro and Halima, made their way to the elevators. All were well bundled up with thick coats, scarves, hats, boots, and gloves. Some held preschool reading workbooks in their reusable grocery bags.

"Whoa," remarked Vadim. "What kind of a mob is this?"

Jethro answered, "No need to get all excited. Just a throng of tutors, heading to the community centre."

"Tutors?"

Jethro explained, "I hope you saw the e-mail which I have sent this morning, asking for volunteers to do some community work. Half of us will help high school students with their homework while the other half will assist with the Adult Literacy Program."

Halima added, "Some of us have invited friends and family members to help out."

Vadim snickered, "Oh yeah, that e-mail. You may be wondering what those dummies have been doing during their lifetimes..."

There was a sudden silence as everyone glared at Vadim disapprovingly. One burly Native man stepped forward heavily. Vadim's humour turned into fear.

"Paul—" began Jethro.

"I'll be brief, Jethro." Paul turned to Vadim. "Listen to my story. Since I was a kid, my dad didn't want any one of us kids to go to school because he was afraid that we were going to be smarter than him. To add to his hardened rule, he banned all books, music, and games from the house. He made us work on the farm all day and spent much of his time on booze. If any one of us made a mistake, he would laugh at us, call us a dummy, and beat us with his walking stick. Luckily, my mom secretly requested our babysitters to teach us. My dad was finally hauled off to a mental institution miles away from our farm. My mom then sold the farm for a very generous price and we moved into a cosy apartment next to a community centre where my siblings and I received free tutoring. I was ten years old with a Grade 1 reading level, but within months I excelled well enough to be placed in sixth grade. The story was similar with my brothers and sisters. If it weren't for my mother, her friends and our tutors, we would still be treated like dummies by my father. Bottom line is, if you insult anyone still learning how to read and write, you're also insulting me big time." He picked up Vadim by the front of his shirt until their eyes met. "Get the picture?"

Vadim nodded timidly. "Sorry about the bad joke. I really am."

When Paul lowered Vadim, one pair of elevator doors opened.

Vadim said, "I-I-I have something else to do. I'll see you guys tomorrow."

As Vadim hurried away, Jethro declared, "Okay, everyone, let's get going. Those who can't squeeze in, we'll meet you at the lobby."

When a few persons decided not to congest the elevator, the doors closed.

Covering their faces with a reading workbook, Halima remarked, "I knew Vadim would say something like that."

Jethro nodded. "I know. I'm glad Paul stepped up to teach him a lesson. Not exactly the way I would want, but it will do. He will learn one day that the focus of life shouldn't always be on himself, but more importantly, on those around him." Jethro sighed. "I do admit, however, the sooner the better."

"YOU WAIT right here and I'll bring Jethro out to meet you," said Halima at the elevators on the following day.

She was about to enter the department when she heard Vadim's voice. "Hey, who invited this bum here?"

She rolled her eyes upward. "Oh, no."

She beckoned two men at the photocopier. "Hey, guys. Vadim's out there, harassing Jethro's guest. Please keep him under control."

"Will do," chorused the men as they headed out the door.

Soon Halima brought Jethro to a shouting match between Vadim and two coworkers. Behind them, a scruffy-looking man with tangled hair, dressed in torn clothes and a dirty red toque, cowered against a wall.

"Leave the man alone, Vadim!" ordered one coworker.

"How can a dumb bum like that piece of trash have a decent appointment with our manager?" demanded Vadim.

"It's none of your business, Vadim!" shouted the other colleague.

Jethro separated Vadim from the men while Halima approached the guest.

She put her arms around him. "It's okay, Frank. Jethro will help you."

"I shouldn't be here," the man named Frank said.

"No, that's not true. You have the right to be here."

Jethro demanded, "Vadim, what's the meaning of this racket?"

Vadim pointed at the stranger. "That dumb bum ridiculously claims that he has an appointment with you at noon."

"And you didn't believe him?"

Vadim was shocked. "What? Why are you letting—"

"Right now I want you to remember that all humans are to be treated with respect, no matter how they appear. Insulting is not the way to show courtesy. This kind of behaviour will bring this company down if you don't think through what you have said and done. I can't make you to apologize like a parent disciplining a kid, so whether or not you apologize will be up to you."

To the employees, he ordered, "Gentlemen, take him back to his desk."

One nodded. "Yes, Jethro."

The other added, "With pleasure."

Taking him by his arms like arresting policemen, they escorted Vadim away from the elevators.

Jethro approached his guest and bent down. "Frank, it's okay. I'm sorry about the whole thing. We didn't expect you to bump into Vadim."

"Maybe we should meet another day."

Jethro shook his head. "No, we need to do this now for your sake. Let's get you up."

Jethro and Halima assisted Frank to his feet. The manager quickly glanced at his sleeves.

"Halima, would you please do me a favour and get the coat and hat from my cloak closet in my office? My wallet is in there."

"I'll be right back."

LATER IN THE AFTERNOON, Vadim was sitting at his desk with his fingers drumming lightly. On his computer monitor, a message blinked endlessly: "Unable to retrieve program. Please contact your Tech Administrator." Once in awhile, he looked around. If someone saw him, that person would either look away or give him an accusatory look. Vadim returned his attention to his screen.

Soon a young man hurried to Vadim. "Hi, I'm Francis. Sorry for the delay. It's unfortunate that I got into an elevator that needed to stop at every floor."

Vadim flapped his hands upward. "Okay, just take a look at my monitor and do your stuff."

With one glance at the monitor, Francis opened a few system-related folders. He clicked a program and typed a series of commands. He restarted the computer and stepped back for Vadim to log-in when the system was ready. Within moments, Vadim was able to reactivate the programs without any problem.

"Wow, you have a magic touch, Francis. Thanks. Hope I can return the favour."

"There is one this you can do."

"What's that?"

"Stop referring to me as a dumb bum."

Startled, Vadim looked around but Francis was already gone.

That was him? he thought. That dirty scumbag Frank is now Francis?

TWO DAYS LATER, Vadim was rushing to Jethro's office clutching a file folder to his chest. He was a few steps away when he stopped abruptly. On the first door was a paper sign which read "Donation Station." Below it was a Missing Child poster. Stepping in, he watched as two women took clothes out of bags, folded them, and placed them in large plastic bins. In a corner were stacks of blankets, pillows, and sleeping bags.

One woman greeted, "Hi, Vadim. Welcome back."

The other said, "I hope you enjoyed your two days off."

Vadim looked ahead at Jethro's office. Another sign covered Jethro's name on the door. It read, "Food Pantry (Non-Perishable, please)."

A voice behind him called, "Excuse us, Vadim. Coming through."

He stepped away as a few coworkers brought in bags of food into the pantry. He followed the last person and glared in astonishment. They took the food from the bags and sorted them into labelled bins, such as "Canned Goods," "Pasta," "Cereal," "Condiments/Spices," "Baby Food Items," "Pet Food," "Bottled Drinks," and "Snacks."

Vadim tapped a man's shoulder. "Hey, where are Jethro and Halima?"

"Oh, you know where Kim and Dave used to sit before they left the company two months ago?"

Vadim rushed around the floor until he saw Jethro and Halima at their new desks. Puzzled, he approached them.

Noticing Vadim, Jethro whispered, "Get ready."

Vadim demanded, "How can you let just anyone oust you out from your offices?"

Jethro replied, "We're not forced out. We volunteered our offices. We're happy with our new desks, where we can get close to you guys."

Halima remarked, "Looks like someone didn't read the e-mail you forwarded two days ago, Jethro."

Before Vadim could talk back, Jethro explained, "The management of the building felt a change was needed for the annual Christmas giving. Instead of choosing a needy family to support through gifts and necessities of life, each business is to set up a year-round donation storage. Whenever we want to, we'll take supplies to all the shelters, drop-in centres, and food banks in the downtown area."

Halima added, "I just heard that Oscar is planning to turn his office into a drop-off depot for toys and books. He'll be moving to Stacy's desk, who's now a stay-at-home mom."

Jethro chuckled, "He loves her desk. He prefers corner spaces."

Vadim couldn't believe the explanation. "And everyone is following this crazy idea?"

Halima pointed out, "It's voluntary. And yes, just about everyone is pitching in. And yesterday a few people came out with new ideas."

Jethro declared, "If you need to discuss this further, we can do so at lunchtime. Now, is there anything else you need to see me about?"

Lost in his thoughts, Vadim handed the folder to Jethro. The manager looked at its contents and smiled. He returned the folder.

"Very good. Our profits are steady. We got more new clients."

Halima nodded. "I heard different departments are hiring more people at entry level."

"Do you still want to discuss our new donation station?"

Still confused, Vadim answered, "No thanks. I'll find that e-mail."

As Vadim departed, Paul and a woman approached Jethro's and Halima's desk. Halima declared, "Well, if it isn't Paul and Zillah, the Sandwich Run Committee leaders."

Vadim asked, "Sandwich Run Committee?"

Ignoring him, Zillah reported, "Since I sent the e-mail yesterday, the response was overwhelming. We just finished making twenty various sandwiches. Paul brought in lots of chocolate bars and a case of twenty-four juice boxes. Francis, who is busy at this moment, collected over fifty restaurant gift cards. Right now, four people are putting together lunches into lunch bags and two are stuffing dog biscuits into resealable bags."

Paul added, "At lunchtime, Francis, myself, and two other people will load the lunches and as many blankets, pillows, and sleeping bags as we can from the Donation Station into my SUV and give them to all the street people we can find. Of course, those with dogs, we'll give them the dog biscuits."

Jethro declared, "That's awesome progress. Good work."

As he headed towards his desk, Vadim muttered, "Sandwich Run Committee?"

AS HE STEPPED out of the building and into the snowy outdoors later that day, Vadim noticed Jethro walking two blocks ahead.

Strange. Jethro usually drives to work. He's walking the wrong direction.

Hoping not to be discovered, Vadim followed Jethro. At every block, he watched as his manager gave money to beggars. Once in awhile, Jethro stopped to talk to some who seemed familiar to him.

How can he be friends with the dirtiest lowlifes? Vadim asked himself. He couldn't believe his eyes as Jethro continued to walk. What? He's not taking the subway? He already passed the station.

Vadim became more shocked as Jethro entered the poorest area of downtown. Old houses tried to look their best with Christmas decorations despite their rundown appearance. Small shops, restaurants, and clinics appeared as a sharp contrast to their dreary neighbouring buildings. Graffiti didn't help much to brighten up the area. People huddled to keep themselves warm at just about every manhole cover and sewage grate.

Why would a guy like Jethro come into a neighbourhood like this?

Vadim felt appalled as Jethro walked into a housing project. At the doorway of one of the apartments stood a group of kids with their stuffed hockey bags, helmets, and sticks. They cheered as Jethro slowly walked through them.

"Okay, team," declared Jethro. "Glad to see you ready. Give me about fifteen minutes to change and I'll meet you out here."

The kids quieted down as Jethro disappeared through the main doors.

Vadim stood in disbelief at the far end of the sidewalk. *Jethro lives here? How did he become poor?*

ON THE FOLLOWING day, Vadim found Jethro in the staff kitchen, watching the coffee percolate. He approached his manager.

"Jethro, may I ask you something?"

The manager sighed. "I figure you're going to talk to me about yesterday. I saw you following me. Yet, I don't think your action would be enough to be considered stalking."

Vadim scratched his head. "How did you end up in a place like that dump? Did you lose a lot of money in a bad investment?"

"Vadim, I didn't end up in the housing project because of bad choices. Rather, I chose to live there."

"What? What about that mansion?"

"I sold it. It's too big for me to take care of. I don't have enough possessions to fill every room. In case you're going to ask about my Rolls Royce, I traded it for a smaller, gas-efficient used car."

"Okay, how about that motorboat at the marina?"

"Sold that, too."

"That nice cottage near a beach up north?"

"Sold that to my current tenants. They're going to run it as a bed-and-breakfast business."

"How did you get to live in that rundown accommodation?"

"I have a friend who is part of the committee who looks after living places and other necessities for those with very low income or none at all. They're in desperate need of a part-time assistant who will help to oversee the people in that apartment complex. The problem is they don't have the money to pay the person. I told him that I'll take the job for free in exchange for accommodation and they can charge me just seventy-five percent of the usual rent. If they need to charge me fully, so be it."

"Why are you doing this?"

"Simple. I care about people and I'll do the best I can to help them live sufficiently."

Vadim started to walk out of the kitchen. "I don't understand how you can waste your money and time on losers like them."

"Careful, Vadim. You don't even know who are included as ones whom you called losers."

Vadim glared at Jethro before heading off.

LATER, HALIMA was setting up coffee, tea, and snacks in a boardroom. Finding her there, Vadim entered the room. She glanced at him without stopping her preparations.

"Vadim, I can allow you to stay here for a few minutes before Jethro and the team leaders come in."

"That's fine. I only need to discuss something with you."

She placed a meeting agenda in front of each chair. "Jethro told me about your talk. I have to be honest. I can't believe how arrogant you are."

He was surprised to hear her words. "Arrogant? My dear lady, you don't even know what you're saying. Our boss is throwing away money, time, and prestige to people who can't even take care of themselves."

She placed her hands on her hips. "Jethro was hoping his actions would not be known throughout the company. Since your curiosity has gotten the best of you, I do believe he wouldn't mind me telling you his secret. Just promise us not to gossip to everyone else."

Vadim nodded. "Now we're getting somewhere."

She heaved a sigh. "Vadim, while Jethro was away for weeks, how did you think our company managed to bounce back financially without facing pink slips and bankruptcy?"

He thought for a moment. "Maybe someone went to some wealthy tycoons for a big bailout."

She shook her head. "We didn't get any outside help. Not a millionaire. Not the head of the city's financial corporation. Not the mayor. Not even the reps of provincial and federal governments. Jethro took the matter into his own hands and stabilized the company's finances."

He glared at her. "How did he do it? The money this company needed to get onto its feet might have been in the hundred of thousands. How did he get the money? His bank accounts might not be enough."

"He did sell three big possessions, among many other things, didn't he?"

His eyes widened in astonishment. "His mansion, his motorboat, and his cottage. He also traded cars."

She nodded. "Now you're starting to get the picture."

"Why did he sacrifice so much for us?"

"I do believe he told you these words: 'I care about people and I'll do the best I can to help them live sufficiently.' When he said 'people', he didn't just mean the homeless or those living in shelters or the housing projects. He also included us."

He sighed. "Just clarify for me one more thing. When did he decide to do this great big sacrifice?"

"Two weeks before his absence. He received an e-mail from the president that our company would be facing massive layoffs. You know, at that time, we didn't sell much of our products and we had a huge debt from one of our creditors; that company had threatened us with a potential lawsuit if we didn't come up with the money fast enough. The following week, rumours about unemployment spread around here like wildfire. Jethro hated to see the company plummeting to nothing and everyone having an unhappy outlook on their lives. The president tried to tell him not to do anything, but Jethro loved the company too much not to back down."

Vadim thought for a moment. "Halima, I kinda did a quick mental calculation and, please correct me if I'm wrong . . . but Jethro did one more thing to keep the company going."

She nodded. "While everyone else got a raise, he insisted on a paycut and ordered me not to follow suit."

"By how much?"

"I don't know. All I can estimate is how much he wanted."

"And that is?"

"A little more than entry level."

Shocked by the revelation, Vadim fled out the boardroom. Arriving at his desk, he landed hard on his chair. Those near him were startled at his commotion.

One called, "Hey, Vadim, are you okay? Looks like something spooked ya."

"I'm fine. Thanks."

Another asked, "Do you need anything to calm you down?"

"No, thanks. I just need to relax and I'll be okay when I get back to whatever I was doing in front of this monitor."

Still another asked, "You're sure?"

"Yeah, I'm sure. Thanks."

He stared at his monitor as if he was analyzing a client's file. However, his mind was burdened by his conversation with Jethro.

"I don't understand how you can waste your money and time on losers like them."

"Careful, Vadim. You don't even know who are included as ones whom you called losers."

He buried his face into his hands. *I should have known better.*

JETHRO POKED his head through the open window. "Three more dinners. One turkey dinner, one roast beef, and one vegetable casserole."

Six of his staff inside the kitchen chorused, "Yes, Jethro."

Jethro and some of his staff were serving dinners in the community near to the housing project. The dining hall was decked with every kind of Christmas trinket, whether bought or handmade. The manager acted as the head waiter, glancing at a line of people who were waiting to be seated. Beside him were three women, including Zillah, and one man holding empty trays. At one corner, three persons were slicing various cakes. At another corner with a Christmas tree, Paul stood behind a counter as if he was a bartender, pouring out juice into cups. Behind him were canisters of coffee and hot water. Francis with a wet cloth and another young man holding a large garbage bag waited at another corner. At one end of each long table, a community volunteer acted as table host as they watched for patrons leaving the table. The rest of the room was filled with people enjoying their meals.

From the kitchen, a man announced, "One turkey dinner, one roast beef, and one vegetable casserole! Ready to be served!"

Zillah declared, "I'll take them."

Jethro instructed, "To Table 3."

A small family stood up at one table. They gathered their coats and belongings. As they left their table, they thanked all the volunteers they saw. At that point, Francis and his clean-up partner cleared the now empty places.

The community volunteer at the table held up four fingers towards Jethro. To the waiting people, he called, "Okay, next four persons, please come and take your places at Table 2."

After two men and a woman with a child were escorted to their chairs, Jethro turned to see a young bearded man in a wheelchair. He already had his tray laid across the armrests. Bags of stuff hung on the handles behind him.

Jethro shouted, "Table 6 or Table 7, is there room to put this gentleman at the end?"

The host at the very last table replied, "There's room for him!"

Jethro walked to the back of the wheelchair. "Allow me."

"Thanks, man."

Jethro pushed the wheelchair to the empty spot at the final table.

Everything seemed to proceed smoothly until one of the servers dropped a tray of drinks onto the floor.

"Sorry, Jethro!"

"No problem! Can someone get a mop?"

A voice from the dining entrance called, "Got it!"

Jethro was surprised. "Vadim!"

All the office staff watched in awe as Vadim, with his coat, gloves, and hat on, wheeled in a pail of soapy water. He held a long mop. As the server picked up the cups, Vadim dunked the mop into the pail, wheeled it through the wringer back and forth, and then mopped up the spilled liquid.

Jethro carefully approached him. Vadim sheepishly explained, "Uh, hi. I did a lot of thinking during my break and I figured it's time for me to make my contribution to this community."

Jethro smiled. "It's good to see you here."

"Thank you. I figure I have to give up one thing that may be bigger than my money and time."

"What's that?"

"My pride."

Jethro chuckled lightly. "Keep up the good work. As soon you're finished, put away your coat and gloves in a corner of the kitchen and leave the mop with Francis. Once you're ready, I'll send you to help Michelle with the donated clothes in the next room."

"Sure thing. Thanks for being an example for all of us."

After Jethro slapped him on the back, Vadim continued with the clean-up.

"We know what love is because Jesus gave his life for us. That's why we must give our lives for each other."

—1 John 3:16 (CEV)

Bonus

I included this Easter-themed story, which I never had the time to turn into a card. I wrote it sometime after my first Christmas story and recently rediscovered it. Once again, it's a Scrooge-like tale. In a sense, it mirrored God's love for everyone, whether their relationships with others were good or not, and He showed His grace at the expense of His Son.

What Would Satisfy the Mistress of Misery?

THE SMALL VILLAGE OF Kammar might be a nice place to live if it weren't for Frieda McInter, whom the folks called the Mistress of Misery. She made her business by loaning money to desperate people in need. She added a large extra fee to every loan paid back. The people sought to appease her by giving her some of their possessions, which might decrease the amount of their loans . . . slightly. It nearly got to the point where she put the whole village into bankruptcy.

She opened all the windows wide—even in the winter—because she wanted every person to hear her ranting at her unfortunate "clients."

"You miserable idiot! This is the sixth week you're late with your payment! You know it will cost you twelve times the original loan!"

"I'll take your ridiculous-looking jewellery case! I will deduct what you originally owe me by ten percent! Nevertheless, you are seven weeks behind!"

"I don't care if your business has been slow lately! You should know better how to run it! If you don't have the money ready by next week, I'll take over your business and anything else that can cover your five-month loan!"

Whenever people saw her coming, they avoided her as if she carried a serious virus. They would quietly criticize her.

"It's no wonder she never has company. All her relatives left the village years ago. She never made a friend and no man dares to be her lover."

"I never seen her smile. Even if she does, I'd hate to think why."

"She even thinks Dickens' *A Christmas Carol* is a big joke. She probably considers Scrooge a wimp."

Frieda didn't care about the comments, but if she recognized a voice as one of her borrowers, she would consider increasing the loan.

ONE WINTER DAY, a man came to see Frieda. The old woman, wrapped in numerous blankets in spite of the burning fireplace, sneered at him, but he tried not to appear intimidated.

Showing respect, the man removed his hat. "Ms. Frieda, I—"

"Enough of the greetings, Hubert! I know why you are here!"

"I'm afraid I won't be able to pay you back for another month. I just bought medicine needed for my son's illness."

"I have to wait a month for the money? I hope that medicine will be enough for your son to survive!"

"The money will be enough to pay the entire loan."

"Well, I hope so! I have little patience with missed payments!"

"Yes, ma'am, I certainly am aware of it."

After he left, Hubert saw a little girl running towards him. "Papa! Papa! Come home, quick!"

Hubert bent down to her eye-level. "What's wrong, Ianna?"

"Lazaro has fallen ill. Mama has taken him to the doctor."

Hubert was dumbstruck. "Oh no."

DR. QUIZO SHOOK his head. "There is not much I can do. I'm sorry."

Hubert, his wife, and daughter stared at him in disbelief. Hubert's wife pleaded, "Please, Doctor, there must be something you can do. And what about the medicine we finally got for him?"

"Lazaro is dying, Tanya, and the medicine will only do very little to help him. An operation wouldn't help. He has less than a month to live."

Tanya and Ianna embraced Hubert dearly and fearfully. He rubbed their backs gently in an effort to console them.

Dr. Quizo spoke up, "Oh, yes. Lazaro would like to discuss something with you, Hubert. You can see him now."

Hubert slowly entered the room. He gazed at his son, who was lying on the only hospital bed. Next to him was a chair. He walked over to his bedside and sat on the chair.

Lazaro slowly turned his head. "Papa?"

Hubert laid his hand on his son's hand. "I'm here, Lazaro. Dr. Quizo said that you wanted to talk about something with me."

The boy nodded. "Papa, before I begin, I need you to promise me one thing."

"What is it?"

"No matter what the outcome will be, will you not refuse or change my request?"

"I promise, Son. Despite what our family has been through, you are the one with a good heart for everything and everyone. I'm proud of you."

"DR. QUIZO, THIS better be the truth!!" shouted Frieda.

A week later, Frieda had fallen unexpectedly ill and called the good doctor to examine her. He studied the results in her little bedroom where she lay on her bed.

"I'm telling you the truth, Ms. Frieda. You will not be able to live for another week without an operation. All your organs are failing and your blood, well, is rather weak."

"I hope you're not saying this so you can get a decrease in your loan!"

Quizo glared at her. "Ms. Frieda, my job is to make people better as best I can. That's all."

"Oh, I might as well go along with you to the hospital and get myself operated upon!"

"That is not going to be easy. You don't have any family or close friends."

"What? To pay my hospital bill?!"

Quizo shook his head. "To test whether their organs and blood are compatible with your body. Because of the way you treat others in the village, finding a willing donor is not going to be easy. I'm sorry, but unless you change your ways and become more friendly than business-like, I'm afraid your chance of survival is slim."

"You will find a donor, won't you?"

He shrugged. "I'll try my best. Like I have said, it's not going to be easy."

Dr. Quizo picked up his medical bag. He was heading out the door when Frieda called, "Doctor?!"

He turned.

"Don't you get your hopes up about your loan!"

"Of course not. Good day."

When he closed the front door behind him, Dr. Quizo found himself confronted by many village people. They appeared anxious and determined.

"Well, Doc, what did you find about that Lady Scrooge?"

"Please, don't speak harshly about her. You'll make matters worse for yourselves."

"You're not going to make her well, are you, Doc?"

"As soon I find her a donor for her needs, she will be better."

"You mean she'll be worse! If you operate on her, she'll be back to her old self and make our lives even more miserable!"

"I'm a doctor. My job is to make people well as best I can. That includes Ms. Frieda. I treat her with the same attitude as I do all of you. Besides, if I were to make her well, it's up to Ms. Frieda to decide how she'll live. It's the same for all of you."

"Dr. Quizo!"

A nurse pushed her way through the crowd. She handed a small note to him. Reading it quickly, his eyes showed urgency.

He hurried away from Frieda's house. "Oh, no."

STANDING BEFORE a hospital room, Dr. Quizo looked at Hubert, Tanya and Ianna. "Are you sure?"

Hubert glanced at his family. "Yes, let us see her."

The doctor gently knocked on the door. He opened it and let the family in. Hubert guided Tanya and Ianna into the room. Resting in bed was Frieda. Her eyes slowly opened in suspicion as the family came closer to her. The little girl hid behind her mother.

Frieda sneered, "Be glad I can't raise my voice like I normally do. I didn't think I would be here so soon since the doctor gave me the sad outlook about my life two weeks ago."

Hubert explained, "We're here to see how you are feeling."

"My question is, why are you here? Also, what's your business with my operation?"

Tanya replied, "We're here to see you. How do you feel?"

"You're hoping to convince me to let you delay your loan, isn't that right?"

Hubert shook his head. "To tell you the truth, we're here because our son has given you a gift for your operation."

"Where is that sick-looking boy of yours?"

Tanya answered, "He was the reason why you are alive. He has given you everything he was."

"I don't understand. You're talking in riddles."

Hubert explained, "The day before your surgery, he died. After his death, his organs and blood were transplanted into you. He was the perfect match for you."

Frieda snickered weakly, "You convinced him to give up his organs for me, didn't you?"

Hubert shook his head. "No, he asked me to promise him not to change or refuse his request. His request was to literally give away any part of him to whoever was in need. He didn't exclude anyone, not even you."

The Mistress of Misery was in deep thought. "Oh, my. This gift goes beyond the value of your loan. In fact, it may cover everyone's debt."

Tanya pointed out, "How could you put a price on someone's life, especially on the one who gave his all to you? You can't possibly estimate the cost of someone's generosity. It's too big to pay, but it isn't to receive."

Frieda asked, "What about my business?"

Ianna peeked behind her mother. "It is finished."

Hubert proudly patted his daughter's head. "Indeed. The best thing for you to do is to consider what to do with your new life."

THE GREEK WORD TETELESTAI MEANS "IT IS FINISHED." IN THE SAME WAY, WE HAVE A DEBT THAT IS IMPOSSIBLE TO PAY; THE "DEBT" INCLUDES ALL OUR WRONGDOINGS THROUGHOUT OUR LIVES. WITH THIS DEBT, IT IS IMPOSSIBLE TO GO TO HEAVEN. HOWEVER, JESUS CHRIST PAID THE PENALTY BY DYING ON THE CROSS AND ROSE FROM THE DEAD SO THAT WE ALL GO TO HEAVEN. IT IS HIS GIFT TO US ALL; ALL WE NEED TO DO IS ACCEPT IT. "JESUS SAID, 'IT IS FINISHED.' WITH THAT, HE BOWED HIS HEAD AND GAVE UP HIS SPIRIT" (JOHN 19:30, NIV). IT IS FINISHED.

THE DEBT HAS BEEN PAID.

HOW SHOULD YOU LIVE YOUR LIFE?

What's Next?

I WILL CONTINUE my tradition, touching on other topics which deal with the needs (physical, emotional, etc.) of people. I know some subjects are a bit touchy to some readers, so I hope that the way I compose them will not irate them, but encourage them to at least think otherwise.

I hope these stories will encourage you to live your lives to their fullest and think of ways to help others. Besides, one has to remember:

> *"He who pursues righteousness and love*
> *finds life, prosperity and honor."*
>
> —Proverbs 21:21 (NIV)

I wish you Season's Blessings, not only during Christmas, but throughout the whole year.